MIST

For Henri and my boys,
OJ and Jordan, and for Mandy

The Curse of the Lost Girls

Listen, my children. Have you heard of the Lost Girls? They go into the woods and never come back.

There was Daisy Gunn who dropped her red mitten, and ran back to find it as the sun went down. She was never seen again!

And Polly Hawk with her fancy ways. She flaunted into the mist beneath the trees and was gone.

Or poor Milly Suggs, who went picking violets. Next evening she came staggering out, hair as white as snow, back bent, the basket of violets turned to dust – a little old lady, her life gone in a night and day.

It's the Elf-King's curse! Beware of it, my daughters. Stay close to Mama.

Old Wives' Warning
By Druscilla Church, British Folklore Society

One

Don't go into the wood after dark. Her mother's warning echoed in her head, but Nell ignored it.

Shadows flickered in the corner of her eye and the trees creaked and groaned in the cold wind, making the hairs on the back of her neck stand up in alarm. The wood was ancient. It spread out for miles behind her house, dark and secretive. If she stared into it, it seemed to stare back. If she ran down the narrow paths, branches grabbed at her like twiggy hands.

She was heading for the darkest part of all, where the ground dropped into a hollow and the path became stepping stones over marshy ground. It used to have an iron fence all the way round, but recently someone had torn it down.

Mist filled the hollow like smoke in a dish and never went away. The dampness caused the trees all around to

1

be covered with ivy and mosses that hung like hair from the branches. As she walked down the slope into the mist, she began to think she could hear a ghostly music, right on the edge of her hearing, as though someone was playing something old-fashioned, like a harp.

That wasn't all she could hear. Somewhere in the woods something was howling. A thousand years ago it would've been a wolf, now it was probably a Staffie belonging to one of the boys who liked to think they were gangsters. They brought the dogs into the woods to train, making them dangle off branches by their teeth, and then wielding them at people like weapons. Hopefully the warden who patrolled the woods would go after them and not notice her.

She was following someone else. Her mystery boy.

He was somewhere ahead of her, very close. He was the reason she was creeping through the trees, instead of at home, out of school uniform, enjoying tea and a little Princess Zelda.

She jumped on to the first stepping stone, the mist swirling around her and settling on her face like tiny pearls. Then on to the next. There were twenty stones across the bottom of the hollow, the ground either side soggy and covered in brambles. She had a brief vision of falling and breaking her ankle. Would anyone think to look for her down here? No, because hardly anyone came this far. She would die a lonely, painful death, and Gwen, her sister, would hang a school scarf and a bunch of flowers from a nearby tree, a sad reminder of a young life lost. Although if it happened to Gwen then there'd be a whole bank of flowers and little messages from her sobbing friends saying Rest in Peace Angel, we all miss you.

She reached the last stone and stopped. Mystery boy had disappeared. That was impossible – she'd seen him walk into the mist, skipping oddly from stepping stone to stepping stone as though he'd decided to play a complicated game of hopscotch. So where was he? Unless he was brambleproof or he'd sunk in the mud, he should be ahead of her.

A twig snapped like a gunshot.

'Nell Church?'

She froze. He was behind her and that wasn't in the plan. He wasn't supposed to actually see or speak to her. She prayed for invisibility or the end of the world, whichever was quicker, but it didn't happen. So she turned around and he was there, vivid in the twilit mist. How many fourteen-year-old boys had skin as pale as milk as though they'd never seen the sun, hair so white it looked bleached and eyes as black as charcoal? Add to that the small silver earring glittering in one ear, and the small tattoo of a wolf's head on the inside of one of his skinny white wrists. Who *was* he?

'If you wanted to ask me out, you could've done it at school,' he said, with his crooked grin, the one that drove her crazy. His accent wasn't local, it was singsong and breathy, maybe a little bit Irish or Scottish, but not really like either. He just sounded like no one else she knew.

He'd started at Woodbridge Community College last week, and it seemed that no one except her noticed that he hardly attended any lessons. Instead he spent his time watching the Woodbridge students as though he was a prince and school was a strange ritual he'd never come across before. And the more no one noticed him, the more he started showing off, rolling out of cupboards during maths lessons or walking across the stage during assembly. His face and name slipped out of everyone's mind, except hers. All she knew was that each morning he came out of the woods and each afternoon he went back in there. Her house backed on to the woods, and she'd watched him from her bedroom window, wandering out in the mornings, yawning and leaning over the fence to pinch an apple from the neighbour's tree. Then in the afternoon he'd go running and leaping back down the bramble-covered paths as though he couldn't wait for the woods to swallow him again.

'Sorry, I wasn't, I didn't . . .' she began.

'Joking,' he said.

She felt a blush start to storm up her face. 'Oh. Of course.'

A silence fell. Top of the class, yet she couldn't think of one single thing to say to start a conversation. Unlike Gwen, who failed all exams but who'd happily chat away to an alien if one landed and was cute enough.

'Don't you know it's dangerous near the mist?' he said. 'People disappear and are never seen again.'

He was teasing her. Maybe she deserved it for following him so clumsily.

'And don't you know the woods are private?' she said, grasping at straws. 'You'll get done for trespassing.' Stupid, ridiculous thing to say. Did he look like the sort of boy who would care? No.

He jumped a stepping stone closer, gazing at her through his spiky fringe, head angled to one side. 'Woods don't belong to anyone, except Gaia.'

'If that's another name for Woodbridge Council, then yes,' she said.

He laughed, which was something. Usually no one got her jokes. Now he was watching her curiously.

'So why did you follow me?' he said.

She quickly tried to think of a plausible excuse for being here in the wood, with its reputation for being dangerous at night. Not one single idea came to her rescue, so she had to confess the truth.

'If I see something that puzzles me I have to find out about it.'

It was true – not knowing about anything drove her crazy. Maybe she'd inherited a detective gene from her police officer mum, but Gwen claimed it was because she was obsessive. Even as a little girl, if she half saw a street sign or a notice or a poster in the street, she'd *have* to go back and read it all.

'I'm especially attracted to weird or creepy things,' she finished.

The twisty grin appeared again. 'Which am I?'

She concentrated on kicking at one of the white stones. 'Erm. Weird.' She glanced up. He didn't seem bothered she'd just called him a freak. So she carried on. 'I had to find out – who are you?'

He thought about that. 'I'm a boy who doesn't exist,' he said, eventually.

Another silence fell, but it was quickly broken by the sound of someone or something moving through the woods towards them.

6

'Uh-oh,' said Nell, horrified. 'It's the warden.'

She turned and scrambled up the slope, out of the hollow and its cold damp mist. She wasn't like Gwen; she hated getting told off for breaking the rules. The light was dropping quickly, but she saw a shape moving. It wasn't the warden, though, it was something worse. There was a blur of white, swift and low down, then a Staffordshire terrier, all teeth, scars and ragged ears, crashed towards her through the undergrowth and skittered to a halt in front of her, snarling.

'Stay still, don't look it in the eye,' said the boy's voice behind her.

He'd followed her. Immediately the dog turned its attention to him, its lip curling like a wave. The snarling got louder. The boy didn't seem to care.

'Careful,' she breathed, beginning to shake. 'They're trained to attack.'

'I know,' he said.

He lifted a casual hand, pointed a skinny finger towards the dog and said in a calm voice, 'Shush! I'm the boss here. Lie down!'

The dog obeyed straight away. It went down on its belly, flattening itself to the ground, its eyes looking anywhere but at the pointing finger and the boy's gaze. Its snarl turned to a confused whine.

7

'Run.'

'It's not alone,' Nell warned. 'Its owner is—'

She got no farther. Two older boys appeared from between the trees. Nell's heart began to hammer. She knew the face looming towards her, she knew how it could laugh at cruelty to others but would take offence at a moment's notice if someone so much as looked at him wrong. Rikstall, they called him, never any first name. For a moment he stopped, shocked to see the dog lying flat.

'Geddup, Sabre!' he bellowed.

The dog didn't move. Rikstall stormed towards them.

'What've you done to my dog?' he demanded.

He went to the school on the next estate. His school and Woodbridge Community College were rivals. Sometimes two big mobs, one from each, would converge and there would be a fight. Rikstall was always in the middle of it. Nobody messed around with him and his dog.

'I said, what did you do to my dog?' he growled.

The mystery boy turned and stared at him. 'Taught it some manners.'

Rikstall's face didn't change. In one quick movement he'd picked up one of the iron railings from the broken fence, and swung it in a great arc at him. It whistled through the air.

'Watch out!' Nell warned.

The boy half turned. But it was too late. The lethal length of iron was closing fast on its target.

'F'rshak!' he spat.

Quicker than her eyes could follow, his hand moved and suddenly he was holding the iron bar, and Rikstall, older, bigger, meaner, was sucking his fingers like a baby and trying to figure out what had just happened.

Nell began to breathe again, but the victory was short-lived. Suddenly everything went wrong. For a couple of beats the boy stood there, triumphant, holding the railing. Then he gave a cry of pain and dropped the iron bar, clutching his hand as though the metal had become instantly red-hot and burned him. He fell to his knees, his face becoming even whiter in the growing darkness, his eyes screwed shut, his body curled over in pain.

Rikstall's mouth dropped open. 'What's up with him?' He lifted his foot and pushed the boy with his toe. 'Freak.' Then he lifted his foot right back. 'I'll teach him to do stuff to my dog.'

Nell caught her breath. He was going to put the boot in. Thugs like him could never resist the urge to kick someone when they were on the ground. Without thinking, she stepped between them.

'Don't,' she warned. 'Or you'll be sorry.'

Rikstall looked as though he could not believe what was happening to him today. Two people daring to cheek him!

'No, you'll be sorry,' he growled.

He reached one of his great mitts towards her, but at last Nell's mind had started to work. She took a step back and got into her fighting stance, perfectly balanced. Her hands came up.

'Come on, then,' she said, desperately trying to keep her voice from wobbling. 'Who wants a broken leg?'

Rikstall turned and grinned at his friend. 'Did she just say she's going to attack us?' he jeered.

His friend started grinning too.

'Yes, I did.' She bounced on her toes. 'My sensei, Mr Song, taught me a special kick called Heavenly Strike. It's not heavenly though. It's hell. It can snap a thigh bone with one hit. Seriously.'

That amused them. This was turning out to be a fun walk in the woods, they were thinking. One opponent on the floor and now a crazy girl needing to be taught a lesson.

'You're going to take us both on?' Rikstall crowed. 'And you think you're going to win! Bring on the Heavenly Strike.'

'Never said I'd win,' she replied. 'But I will get one

strike in. So one of you will get a broken leg. And lots of pain.' She bounced on her toes some more. 'I mean it. I'm good. One strike and – snap.'

Rikstall's grin died a little. 'Yeah, and then the other one will give you a beating you won't forget, girl.'

She nodded, trying to hide the fact that her knees had now started shaking. 'You're going to punish me anyway. But all the same,' she insisted, 'one of you will be in agony. Who's volunteering?' She pointed at him. 'You, Rikstall? You're the one with the big mouth. Or are you going to make your mate do it?'

They both stared at her.

'Go and shut her up,' said Rikstall.

There was a silence and then, 'You go,' said his friend moodily.

Nell bounced some more. 'Come on, I'm getting cold. Who gets the Heavenly Strike?'

'You dare and I'll—' began Rikstall.

His friend grabbed his sleeve. 'I'm off. This is stupid. Even Sabre's gone.'

It was true – as soon as the boy had collapsed the dog had scurried away.

Rikstall glared at Nell. He jabbed a finger towards her. 'You wait. You and him – next time you won't be so lucky.' He looked down at the boy and went to kick him. He didn't get the chance. The boy looked up.

'Buzz,' he said quietly, still cradling his hand in pain.

Suddenly the humming of a thousand bees filled the air. For a moment Rikstall looked bewildered. The boy's eyes narrowed, his face became sharper. He didn't look like a schoolboy any more.

'Forget about us,' he whispered.

Rikstall and his friend blinked a few times then wandered away through the trees and were lost to the darkness. The buzzing faded away.

Nell breathed out in relief and crouched down beside him. 'You OK?'

His face was now like chalk, but he took a deep breath and got to his knees. 'Yeah. My hand feels like it's going to drop off, but I'll live.'

She sat back on her heels 'Sorry. You got hit trying to help me.'

'Stop apologizing.'

'Sorry – oops.' She grinned sheepishly. 'It's a tic. I've got lots of them.' She held out her hand. 'Let's see the damage.'

He showed her his palm. There was a huge burn mark across it, as though the old iron railing had been red-hot.

'I'm allergic to iron, that's all. Hurts like hell and makes my bones feel as if they're turning to paste.'

He staggered to his feet and she followed. 'It's dark,' he said. 'I'll walk you to the road.'

As they made their way through the trees towards the lights, he said curiously, 'Could you really have broken his leg?'

'Yes.' She liked the fact that he looked surprised. 'Five years of mixed martial arts training,' she explained. 'My mum's a police officer. Do you think I'd get ballet lessons?'

They were nearly at the alley that led from the woods to the main road. Yellow light shone down on them from the streetlights. She stopped and faced him. It was now or never, and she had to know.

'Why have you been watching me and Gwen?' She paused and thought for a moment. 'Well, not so much Gwen because all the boys watch her.' It was true, her sister walked around as though she was on a red carpet with the paparazzi crowding around her. They didn't usually watch *her*. She was a cloud of wild hair on matchstick legs. 'But why me?'

He didn't say anything for a moment. Then, 'No reason,' he said, and turned and disappeared back into the woods.

She stood and watched for a while, then she decided she'd been brave enough for one day. She ran home. She'd reached her front door before she realized he'd called her Nell Church. That wasn't her surname. Church was her father but he couldn't even be bothered to visit so she couldn't be bothered to have his name. She was Nell Beecham, after her mother.

Two

'His name's Evan River,' Nell mused on the morning of Gwen's party. Her cereal was turning to mush in front of her. 'He doesn't even wear the correct uniform. It's as though he's wearing this idea of a school uniform, gold and black but not quite right. Nothing about him is right.'

Her sister put down her eye pencil and looked up from the mirror she'd balanced against the cereal packet, next to the fluttering candle – there'd been another power cut in the night and the town was still blacked out. She gave Nell a withering look. 'There's no new boy. You're making it up because you haven't got a boyfriend.'

'I don't want one. I'm thirteen. I'm not you,' Nell retorted. 'He comes and sits with me at lunch sometimes. We don't talk much.' Just enough for him to give away his name and not much else. She didn't tell her he called her kicking-girl, after that meeting in the woods. Nor did she tell her about the fight. She took out her mobile. 'Look, I took a photo. Even I thought I was imagining him.'

Gwen snatched it and examined the image, her perfect eyebrows rising in surprise.

'Oh my,' she breathed. 'So little sister likes boys with bleached hair, black eyes and wonky smiles.' She angled her head and looked closer. 'Boys who look trickily through their lopsided spiky fringes at you, when they see you taking a snap.' She handed the phone back with a sly smile. 'Out of your league, but well done for trying.' She licked a finger and rubbed a speck of mascara off her cheek. 'Now can we talk about something interesting, like my birthday?'

Nell turned to her mother, Jackie, who was drinking coffee, the phone tucked under her chin, waiting to find out if she had to work double shifts because of the power cuts. She was in her police uniform today, which always worried Nell; she liked it better when her mum did community work, going round to schools, where the worst thing that could happen was a class of motormouth teenagers giving her a hard time.

'I saw him in town, with a skinny dog by his feet. And you know what – the dog was a wolf, I swear.'

'Husky,' said Jackie. 'Beautiful things. So close to being a wolf.'

Nell pushed her bowl away, half eaten. 'Sorry, Mum. But this was a wolf.'

She'd stood in a doorway and watched him. He'd left it outside a jeweller's shop whilst he went inside. It wasn't chained up but just sitting there obediently. Even she had to admit that didn't sound very wolf-like.

'The weirdest thing is that he smells of pine leaves. I smell them in the corridors when he's gone past.'

Nell looked out of the kitchen window, past their untidy overgrown garden to the wood that massed on the other side. The mornings were dark these days, but she could see the outline of the trees, moving in the sharp autumn wind. There were lots of different trees in there, but none of them were pine.

Jackie put the phone down. 'Bad news. Brownhills power station's been hit, which means we've got three more districts without power.' She pulled an apologetic face. 'So I'm on a double shift, girls. Sorry about that.'

'All night?' said Nell doubtfully, whilst her sister raised her arms and did a silent cheer behind her mother's back.

'All night,' said Jackie. 'I'm sorry.' She took her youngest daughter's face between her hands, bunching up

Nell's wild hair, and kissed her soundly on the cheek. 'I know you don't like overnights. But you'll survive this once.'

It wasn't being alone with Gwen in the house that worried her, but Jackie out there in the dark streets, amongst the psychos, the joy-riders and murderers.

'Who's doing this?' said Nell. She hated it when the lights went out. It had been happening all over the country, and now it had hit their town. It turned the familiar streets into something strange and edgy.

'Some group with a grudge. They get in through locked doors, don't trigger the alarms. No one sees anything. Ghosts, probably!'

'Doesn't Dad know who's doing it?' said Gwen. 'He's into that sort of thing, isn't he?'

'If he does, he's not telling me,' said Jackie briefly.

Tom Church was high up in the CID, always working on some important job. He was always too busy to come around and visit, that was certain, which didn't impress Jackie.

'You can ask him the next time he turns up.' She picked up her bag. 'OK. Coats and let's go.'

Nell grabbed the old duffle coat of Jackie's that she'd found in the back of a wardrobe. It was her favourite school coat of the moment. When she wore it she stopped being Nell Beecham and became *Hélène Beauchamp*, kick-ass but beautiful French student, who skipped to school along the left bank of the Seine, rather than Woodbridge Road. No one else thought the duffle looked good, but she didn't worry, because when she was being Hélène nothing bothered her. Which was handy because Gwen was looking her up and down, with her evil alpha-girl face on.

'Isn't it bad enough my mother is a cop without my sister being a weird loner as well?' She put her head on one side and considered. 'I mean, you'd look OK if you let me layer your hair, straighten it and put in some toffee highlights . . .'

'My aim in life is to be the opposite of you,' Nell muttered, but Gwen wasn't listening.

'. . . and pluck your eyebrows.'

'Leave her alone,' said Jackie. 'You don't know everything.'

'I don't know much at all – as my mock exams will soon show,' Gwen agreed. 'But I know about clothes. She looks like a Victorian orphan.'

With that, Gwen put her own coat on – she was the only one who could make the school uniform look hot. She had her black socks over her knees, her skirt was short, her blazer sleeves pushed back, her shirt fitted and tight, her gold and black tie in a loose fat knot. She picked up her messenger bag. 'You're not wearing that to my sweet sixteen tonight,' she warned, as she headed for the door.

'Sweet sixteen? What's she on about?' said Jackie.

'She's having a party in the woods tonight,' said Nell.

Jackie fixed her elder daughter with her official police officer's stare. 'No, she blimmin' well isn't.'

Then the lights came back on.

. . . like other towns and cities across the country, Woodbridge has now suffered its third day of attacks . . . the car radio burbled.

Nell took a black beret from her pocket, looked in the rear-view mirror and pulled it over her wild hair.

. . . perhaps this time the saboteurs have left a clue to their identity. In a bizarre twist, a plane flying over the town during the power cut reported seeing a pattern of lights spelling out the letters F E N across the blacked-out streets . . .

Jackie switched the radio off. It was interfering with the argument she was having with Gwen.

'I'll leave you money for pizza. You're staying in and watching TV.'

'No. I'm having a party!'

'You're staying in and watching TV.'

Nell stared at her reflection and tried to tuck a few curls in, but they wouldn't stay put. Gwen had hair like silk, whilst hers was the opposite. It formed itself into long corkscrew curls and made her look like a lollipop – a great mass of curling hair perched on top of her skinny body, made skinnier by the black uniform and tights she wore with her Docs.

'I can't cancel!' Gwen was howling like a banshee now. 'We've been planning it for weeks.'

Nell ignored them, and had another go at her hair. She'd inherited her curls from Druscilla Church, their gran, who lived on the other side of the woods in a red house with red-stained walls. According to her dad, Druscilla was still wanted by the police for breaking into military bases during the Ban the Bomb sixties.

'You're not getting drunk in the woods with boys. I don't care what the other girls do, you're not.'

'We're camping, that's all.'

'You're not camping. I know what you get up to – sharing sleeping bags, hooking up. I wasn't born yesterday.'

'It's a rite of passage, Mum.'

Nell pulled the beret lower so that it nearly reached her eyebrows and gazed at herself; she had Nan's eyes too, rimmed by dark lashes and with a smokiness to the eyelids as though Gwen had done a really subtle make-up job on her.

'It's getting drunk in the woods and sharing sleeping bags,' said Jackie, finally pulling to a halt in front of the school.

Gwen had the door open before the car had stopped. Immediately a swarm of her friends headed over, all with their uniforms modified to be identical to Gwen's. She was the queen bee, they were her faithful drones. They even smelled the same – green apple chewing gum and cherry lip balm; Gwen probably insisted on it as one of her many rules.

Jackie leaned over and shouted, 'I mean it, Gwen. No woods party. You can have Jake round – but no going off to your bedroom for the whole evening with the door closed, and he doesn't stop the night. I'll be back by eight a.m. tomorrow.'

Gwen popped her head back in. 'You've ruined my life.'

'Shame.'

Gwen waited until her mother had driven away.

'Sorry I told,' Nell said, but Gwen ignored her.

Then she shouted to her friends.

'Hooray for power cuts. Spread the word – the party's on!'

Three

The bell was about to go, but Nell looked round for Evan River.

He wasn't amongst the students filing through the gates, he wasn't amongst the ones sitting on the wall or standing in groups. She'd decided that he must have skipped a day, but then she saw him.

He's definitely not coming to school today, she thought.

He wasn't in uniform. He was on a motor scooter, a Vespa, the engine ticking over. Unbelievably, even by his mysterious standards, he had a small boy perched in front of him, with the same black eyes, the same shape face, the same fine white hair blowing in the breeze. A little brother, maybe. The whole thing was totally illegal – underage, no helmets, riding with a child. Jackie would go insane.

He was watching Gwen and her friends. No surprise there, all the boys looked at Gwen's gang when they flaunted their way into school. They were like a pack of well-groomed salukis, poodles and Lassie dogs with their beautiful hair and sleek make-up.

The bell chose that moment to ring, and she realized she was going to have to walk by him.

That's not a big deal, she told herself. I'll casually go 'Hey', as I go by. Or, 'No school today, lucky you.' Or make a joke, like I've seen Gwen do a million times.

The problem was, that sort of thing came naturally to Gwen, whereas Nell would probably mess it up. It was amazing how she knew the formula for simultaneous equations, but not the one for making friends.

Her steps slowed as she got closer. Worse still – what if she said something and he ignored her? She couldn't risk that because standing by the gate were her two so-called friends Paige and Bria. They were whispering to each other behind their hands and flicking little micro glances at her to see if she'd noticed them ignoring her. Last term they'd been her best mates, but then suddenly, over the summer, they'd morphed into shopping-obsessed, lipgloss-loving, hip-swinging girly girls with boyfriends in tow, and no time for her. They were traitors who told her they weren't going to dance class this term, then joined behind her back. Now every time she saw them she felt like there was a dagger sticking in her heart.

She pushed her hands into her pockets, put her head down, shoulders up, and headed for the gates. Then above the noise of the other students shouting to each other, she heard a voice.

'Hey, Nell.'

Was that Evan? Had he called to her? She carried on walking; she couldn't risk making a mistake in front of Paige and Bria.

'Nell?' It was louder this time.

She stopped and turned around. He wasn't just louder, he was right beside her. He'd scooted the Vespa on to the pavement. If any of the teachers saw him they'd go mad. He didn't look worried though.

'Sorry,' she said. 'Didn't hear you.'

He grinned. 'Saying sorry again.'

She winced. 'Told you. It's a habit. It's like I've got very polite Tourette's.' Two pairs of charcoal eyes surveyed her. 'No school today?' she managed.

'I've been up all night. Working.' He did look tired, with blue shadows under his eyes.

'Didn't the power cuts stop you?'

He seemed to find this amusing. 'The lights going out

don't bother me.'

The little boy was now bouncing up and down and shrieking, 'Whee, whee, come on, let's go!'

Evan pulled a face. 'And now I have to look after this little pest for the day.' He tugged the little boy's hair gently. 'Say hello, Bean.'

The little boy burbled something, then carried on pretending to rev the scooter.

She smiled – she couldn't help it. 'You're the mystery boy and you're baby-sitting?'

For a moment he fiddled with something on the handlebars. She'd noticed before, when she'd been secretly observing him, that his face could change like the wind, going from sulky to happy to tricky in moments. Now he looked fed up.

'Seems like I'm always looking after someone,' he said.

Nell glanced across at her sister. 'Sometimes I feel like that, too.'

For a moment they were in perfect agreement. Then:

'Nell,' said an unwelcome voice.

She came back to earth. Bria and Paige were there, arm in arm. 'Bell's gone. You're going to be late.'

Their words might've sounded friendly, but their eyes were mocking. The dagger in her heart went deeper.

'Why are you even talking to me?' she said awkwardly.

Out of the corner of her eye she could see Evan watching them. Bria and Paige were aware of this too, it seemed. They were tossing their hair about, trying to be alpha girls like Gwen, but they weren't in her league.

'Jeez, Nell,' said Paige, sweetly. 'We were only going to say sorry we laughed when you got your hair caught in the car door yesterday!'

They both exploded into giggles, and then glanced at Evan to see if he'd join their torture group.

'I think there's a few people on the other side of the road who don't know about that,' Nell muttered. 'Perhaps you ought to go and tell them.'

But they'd changed tack, nudging each other and looking Evan up and down.

'He's cute,' said Bria to Paige, as if he couldn't hear.

In Gwen's gang everything was measured in cuteness. If someone or something wasn't high up on the cuteness spectrum, then it didn't exist for them.

To her surprise Evan stared back at them for a couple of beats, then said, 'So why don't you two clear off? We're having a private conversation.'

Nell only just managed to stop her mouth dropping open. Had he really just stuck up for her?

It seemed he had because Paige's eyes went like belt holes, small and mean. 'Oops, I made a mistake. He's *not* cute. He likes Nell, which means he's a loser.'

'Yeah. And should you be riding that?' said Bria, staring at the scooter.

'Should you be minding your own business, perhaps?' he said. He turned back to Nell. 'Who are they?'

'Two girls whose only aim in life is to copy my sister.'

Bria's face became peevish. 'Yeah, that's why we were friends with you, stupid. Because you're Gwen's sister. No other reason.'

The dagger went right in this time and was twisted around. It sometimes seemed to Nell that Gwen got everything. Jackie said that even in her pushchair Gwen'd had a certain way of smiling at total strangers, so they'd come over and give her things. And she'd always managed to get any toys of Nell's that she wanted.

It seemed that now she'd got her friends as well.

To her surprise, though, Evan was ignoring them. He'd still got his charcoal gaze pinned to her.

'Look, there's something important I've got to tell you,' he said. 'I heard your sister. Are you going to the woods tonight?'

'We are,' said Paige, unable to take a hint.

He flicked her an annoyed glance. 'I'm talking to Nell.'

Bria and Paige looked at each other and smirked. 'Talk to us, instead,' said Paige, coyly. 'She's not really the going-into-the-woods sort, but we—'

'Buzz,' said Evan, loudly.

'Buzz, buzz,' mimicked the little boy happily.

Oops, I know what happens now, thought Nell.

And sure enough, flowing around them came the sound of a thousand bees buzzing. It was Rikstall all over again. Bria stopped talking, her mouth at half-cock, then they both picked up their messenger bags, slung them over their shoulders and wandered off through the gates as though they'd forgotten all about their vendetta against her. The little boy waved a tiny hand like a starfish as they went.

When they disappeared, she swung round at Evan.

'How come you can make people forget about you?' she said. 'There's a buzzing noise and then it's as though they've had their minds wiped.'

'You do notice things,' he said.

'Told you. I have to find things out. Maybe I've got detectoring in my blood. So how do you do it?'

'It's a gift,' he said, mock-seriously. 'Even amongst my own people, I'm special.'

'I bet,' she said, straight-faced. 'So why doesn't it work on me?'

He didn't answer straight away.

'You're different,' he said, eventually.

Then the bell went and students began pushing around them, moaning at Evan for taking up room with the scooter. He ignored them. So did Nell. If the whole world had disappeared she probably wouldn't have noticed. What did he mean by *you're different*?

'Don't go into the woods tonight,' he said.

The school entrance had cleared. There was only the two of them, and a silence broken by the little boy on his knee pretending to drive the Vespa and making *brum brum* noises with lots of flying dribble.

Nell hugged her duffle coat around her, suddenly freezing. 'Why are you telling me this?'

He didn't answer. He seemed to be struggling with something inside himself.

'Excuse me – you, yes you, boy!' a voice shouted. It was Foster, the deputy head, bearing down on them. 'Get off the pavement.'

Evan ignored him. 'I don't know,' he said, sounding confused. 'Maybe I shouldn't bother. Except you helped me out, that day in the woods.'

She shrugged. 'It's what all the geeky girls do,' she said, trying to make a joke of it. 'Help strange boys in the woods.'

'And you've got a problem sister.'

What had Gwen got to do with it? 'So?'

'I've got a brother like that.' He looked around, trying to be casual, but she could tell he was nervous about something. 'So please – don't go in the woods tonight.'

'Are you old enough to ride that?' Foster called, as he got closer. 'What's your name?'

They both ignored him this time. 'Why, what'll happen?' Nell had her hand over her heart, which had decided to go into triple time.

He revved the scooter so the little boy clutched the handlebars and laughed excitedly.

Foster pushed her out of the way. 'You can't ride with a child – get off now,' he ordered. 'You're not even wearing helmets.' He squinted at Evan. 'I think you'd better come with me while I check this out.'

Evan ignored him. He scooted forward, so he could see her.

'Please. It's a warning,' he said, and for a moment he didn't look like a baby-sitter, or a schoolboy. He looked like a boy who might live wild in the woods. Then he nodded to her, and roared away in a cloud of blue smoke, the little boy whooping with excitement.

She stood watching the empty road for so long that she was late for registration. It was the first time ever.

31

The Elf-King's Tale

See the chalk-white face at the window, as the storm roars!

It is the Elf-King. Listen as he rattles the latch and tries to get in. How he tries to reach his little daughter in her crib by the fire. Her mother is human, and has taken her from him. What stops him taking her back? Nothing in this world but the horseshoe placed above the door. It is poison to him.

See how he rages and threatens and howls in despair.

'My elskling, my precious, my only kin,' he cries to the baby. 'I cannot reach you!'

Oh, the pity of his chalk-white face against the black sky, and the tears that fall like rain.

'But wait and see!' he rages. 'I will have my revenge on the world of men. I will take your children.'

Then he turns and flees back into the mist. His howls can still be heard to this day, they say.

Traditional Fairytales
By Druscilla Church, British Folklore Society

Four

Druscilla Church stared at Nell.

'You're sure everything's OK?'

'Absolutely, Nan.' Nell crossed her fingers behind her back.

'Hmm.' Her grandmother gave her a lingering look. 'If you say so.' She zipped up her jacket and kicked her motorbike into life. 'And stay indoors. No wandering about. No going into the wood. It's dangerous.' She looked past Nell's house, down the garden to the start of the trees, where moonlight was edging everything with a pale light. 'I don't trust nights when everything looks ghostly.'

With that she drove off down Woodbridge Road, her long, grey plait blowing out like a tail. Nell waved until she disappeared round the corner, and then took the little parcel, still scented with her grandmother's patchouli oil, back inside to Gwen.

'You can stop hiding now. Nan left you a present.'

The ali baba basket of unironed clothes in the corner toppled forward and Gwen crawled out from behind it.

'I thought she'd spotted me with her eagle eyes!' she exclaimed.

Nell stared at her, hand over her mouth, trying not to laugh.

'What?'

'You've got pants on your head.'

They both began sniggering and then laughing, rolling on the floor. Visits from their biker nan affected them like that. She had a way of peering at them as though trying to read their thoughts, especially when they had secrets to hide. It was the one time they were both on the same side.

Eventually Gwen couldn't resist the parcel. She sat up, cross-legged. 'Give me.'

The wrapping paper was ripped off and she held up a steel necklace with lots of odd-shaped stars, moons and other hippy charms hanging from it. On each birthday Nan would give them a necklace, which was handy because Gwen was like a magpie; she loved glittery things.

'Every year, the same thing. But I actually like this

one! Nan – I love you,' she declared, fixing it round her neck and then posing in front of the mirror. She pouted at her reflection, then sighed. 'Although a new mobile might have been better. Does she know they exist?'

'Yes, but she researches fairytales for a living,' said Nell patiently. 'That means little fairy necklaces instead of iPhones.'

Gwen gave herself another satisfied look. 'I'll wear it for the party. It's witchy, like the woods.'

'But you heard Nan say that we're not to go,' Nell insisted.

'She always says that,' said Gwen blithely. 'She's a tree-hugger, a woo-woo. She's always warning us off. I get it. It's taboo.' She smiled excitedly, her eyes sparkling. 'That's why I have to go. Because it's not allowed.'

Nell groaned. 'Mum will go mad when she finds out. Hold the party at someone's house. Or in our garden.'

'No, it has to be the woods. It's so freaky,' Gwen insisted. 'And the warden doesn't patrol at nights.' She fixed her sister with her most innocent gaze. 'Mum's too busy to organize anything for me this year, so this will mean less stress for her.'

'She said we were having a birthday tea on Sunday,' Nell pointed out.

Gwen gave a hollow laugh. 'Yes, with Nan as the star guest! And then Dad'll show up and he and Mum will argue as usual. This is my party.'

Tom Church had left soon after Nell was born. He and Jackie had never married, but Gwen had his surname. According to Gwen, Jackie only fell pregnant a second time to try and keep him from leaving, but it hadn't worked. This made sense to Nell – no wonder she'd been born anxious, all that expectation on her newborn shoulders. It probably explained why her father disliked her too.

Gwen gave a sigh and sat down opposite her. 'Spit it out. What's up?'

She shrugged. 'It's the power cuts. They make everything feel edgy.'

Evan's warning hadn't helped. She'd spent all day puzzling about its meaning, but still couldn't work it out. Did he think that she had any choice? When Gwen decided she'd do something, she did it.

'It could be terrorists doing them,' she finished lamely. 'We should stay in the house, doors locked.'

Gwen rolled her eyes. 'Eejit. You're like this because Mum and Dad are cops. You hear all these bad things and it makes you anxious. You should be like me and take no notice and never watch the news. Half of it's probably smelled of old-fashioned face powder and a little of mothballs. When she came downstairs Gwen looked at her with her head on one side.

'You know what, for someone who looks like road kill most of the time, you sometimes have a stroke of genius. That whole vampire coat thing is so weird it's good, I wish I'd thought of it.'

They met up with the other partygoers at the old church next to the alley. There were over twenty of them sitting on the mossy graveyard wall. Behind them the vicar was standing amongst the overgrown graves, watching them as though they were about to suddenly vandalize something. They were already carrying backpacks full of cider, lager and bottles of vodka, purchased elsewhere by their older brothers and sisters. Alongside the backpacks they were carrying sleeping bags, tents, ponchos and portable speakers.

Bria and Paige were sitting together, arms round their ʙoys. Hanging around the edges of Gwen's gang was ʏing off for them. They didn't exactly get invited to join ʙut the gang liked having adoring followers who hung ʈo their every word and copied everything they did, so ᴡere tolerated.

ʟl sat on her own. In the last few minutes her

made up anyway. Fried food, global warming, terrorists, gangs, drugs – just chill.' She switched on her straighteners and sat tapping them against her knee, waiting for them to heat up. 'You don't have to come. You can lock the doors and watch TV.'

'Not likely,' said Nell. 'If you go, I go.'

Someone had to watch out for Gwen. And that someone was her.

'Yay! Excellent.' Gwen tried to look kindly at her, but it was a hideous attempt. 'I'll straighten your hair for you as a treat. It's like a hedge.'

'I don't want it straightened.'

'Of course you do. Now sit.' She put her hands on Nell's shoulders and forced her down on to a stool. She surveyed her like a professional. 'Do you want it pinned back?'

'No way. It's my shield.'

Gwen tutted like a Geiger counter. 'You hide behind it.'

'Exactly.'

Her sister wielded the straighteners. 'You're lucky to have me, you know,' she declared. 'I help to make you perfect, like me.' Pause. Nell waited for the put-down. 'Or as close to perfect as you're liable to get.'

She sat still as Gwen went to work on her hair. Her

ear got burned several times because Gwen was also sipping from a mug of coffee laced with Jackie's Christmas brandy and shouting instructions to her friends via her mobile on speaker.

'Tell Jake and Jed to get there early and get the tents up. How many have we got? Five? That's enough, we can all squash in. The tighter the better, like sardines. I love being a sardine.'

Nell could hear squeals of laughter and much giggling coming out of the phone.

'I'm not squashing into a tent with you lot and your boyfriends,' Nell said doubtfully.

'You'll be fine.' Gwen took a sip from her mug and pulled a face, then swallowed. 'Stop worrying.'

It took fifteen minutes for Gwen to make any headway on her spiralling, misbehaving hair. When she'd finished Nell went and had a look in the mirror. Her straightened hair was seriously long. She looked like one of the girls in the Pre-Raphaelite paintings they'd seen on their art trip to London; different, older, her eyes in the soft light from the lamp looked as though she'd put make-up on. Her eyebrows, usually in a worried frown, looked less like two stiff caterpillars, and softer.

She looked like the beautiful Hélène Beauchamp. Cool Hélène, who'd been born during one of those awful

outings with their dad, sitting in McDonald's as he stared out of the window, or talked work on his mobile, or argued with Gwen whilst ignoring her.

Gwen rummaged in the laundry basket and held out a top. 'Wear this.'

'No.' Nell didn't even have to look; if it was one of Gwen's she didn't want to wear it. Gwen wore things one size too small so that they fitted her like a second skin.

Her sister rolled her eyes. 'You can't keep walking round with your shoulders hunched, wearing layer after layer of leggings, skirts and jumpers.'

Nell backed away from the skimpy top. 'I can. P look at me weird if I don't wear camouflage.' She'd all her life not competing with her sister. Whatever wore, she wore the opposite.

'They fancy you, that's all,' said Gwen.

'They mock me.'

'That means they *really* fancy you.'

Nell pulled a face. 'Well, I'm not interes'

'You will be.' Gwen looked her up and you won't freeze in that many layers. B coat. I don't want you moaning that y

So Nell went upstairs and dug ou she'd found in the attic when they'd It was soft and dark and came a

stomach had decided to tie itself into knots, and her anxiety levels had gone sky-high. It was as though some part of her, the non-thinking part, had picked up something dangerous in the atmosphere and was trying to tell her to run, run like the wind.

She was about to check her pulse, sure her heart was beating out of rhythm, when someone plonked down beside her.

'Stop sitting there with a thousand-yard stare,' said Gwen. 'Go talk to your friends.'

'They're not my friends any more.'

Gwen shrugged. 'Easy. Get some new friends.'

'I'm trying.' Except he's not your normal Woodbridge boy, she added silently.

'Then be more like me,' said Gwen impatiently.

Hélène broke through. 'Shallow and bitchy?'

'No, fabulous,' said Gwen, hardly listening. She was counting heads. ' I think that's everyone!' Her troops had gathered, she was ready to lead them into the woods.

As if agreeing with her, the clock on the steeple high above them began to chime the hour. She jumped on the wall, clapping her hands.

'OK, people! Thunderbirds are go!'

Before the echoes of the church bell had died away the

whole mob were heading for the woods. Nell let them go, and then trailed after them. The alley leading to the woods was lit by three streetlamps that cast an edgy yellow glow over everything. She walked into the pool of light cast by the first one.

It went out.

She actually heard the little *tink* as the bulb died. She stopped dead. She turned around on her heel, goose bumps breaking out all over. The lights on the road behind her were still on. So were the lights of Rowan House and Beech House, the tall blocks of flats across the road. It wasn't a power cut. Her heart began to thump, but she told herself not to be so stupid. Coincidence, that's all. She stepped quickly out of the shadow and hurried after the last of Gwen's friends as they disappeared over the locked gate at the bottom of the alley and into the wood.

Tink!

As she stepped into the second puddle of light, that one went out too. This time she didn't stop. She carried on, walking rapidly. There was one last lamp at the end of the alley, where the woods began. This one wouldn't go out. That would be stupid and ridiculous.

Tink!

The third bulb popped. Darkness folded over her like velvet. She stopped. She turned around, her heart hammering. And there right in front of her, hanging in the air, was the word NO!

It took her a moment to realize that the letters weren't actually written on the sky, but were the lit windows of the two blocks of flats. The rest of the lights had gone out. There was even an exclamation point of four lit windows down, a space and then another lit window.

A sudden wind blew her hair back. It was scented with pine needles. Evan was close by. She scanned the area. At first she could see nothing, then the fitful moon came out from behind the clouds and there he was, leaning against the wall of one block. Somehow she could tell he was watching her.

Was this his warning? But how could it be, how could he organize the lights to do that?

She glanced away, confused. When she looked back, he'd gone. There was nowhere for him to hide – no bushes, no doorways. He'd either disappeared into thin air or he'd walked through the wall.

Or I'm going crazy, she thought.

A second later all the lights in Rowan and Beech House went out and with them went the warning, as though it had never existed. And then, like some dreadful plague, the darkness began to spread. The lights outside the church went out. And those on the main road, one after

45

another like dominoes going down. Then, as though someone had thrown a switch, the tower blocks in the town centre disappeared. And a moment later the big square block of the police station, where Jackie and her father worked.

Nell couldn't move. She watched it all in horror. In a few moments it was as though the town had gone and all that was left of the world was darkness.

A torch beam suddenly pinned her to the wall in a shining white circle.

She panicked and screamed.

'Nell?' said a voice.

She blinked towards its source, shading her eyes.

'Gwen says please get a move on!' said Jake. 'Well, not exactly those words. You know Gwen-Pottymouth-Church.'

She gave a sigh of relief.

But as she followed him from the blacked-out town into the pitch-dark woods, something close by began to howl.

Five

The howl echoed over the Red House as it cried its tears of blood.

The building had stood next to the woods, a couple of miles from Nell's house, for two hundred years. After each shower of rain streams of red rusty water would pour from its iron window frames, roof and doors, and spurt out of the gutters, staining the grass and bushes that grew around it. A peeling sign at the gate said, British Folklore Society.

Druscilla Church, its current owner, heard the howl. She grabbed a torch and went out of the back door. The wood started at the bottom of the garden. She sat down in the old swing seat on the porch and stared into the dark mass of trees. They were still edged with that ghostly silver that seemed to have nothing to do with the moonlight.

Something was happening out there. She couldn't see

it, but she could feel it. Since she'd got back to the house and parked her Harley, her thoughts had been on Nell. She was sure something was bothering her granddaughter.

A breeze came hurtling out of the wood, smelling not of oak, beech and birch, but of pine needles. She knew there were no pine trees nearby.

The howl came again. She sat bolt upright, her heart pounding. Then she went to the garage and got an iron chain. She wound it round her fist and returned to the porch and sat with it on her knee.

'Fen,' she muttered, into the darkness.

Six

'Feral dog,' said Jake, as they hurried to catch up with the others. 'Probably a Staffie that a gangster boy's turned loose. It won't come near us.'

'No,' said Nell. 'That wasn't a dog.'

A little voice in her head was shouting *danger!* But it made no difference – Gwen was in the wood, so that's where she had to go.

Branches caught at her hair and coat. Unknown creatures rustled in the darkness and scurried through the brambles. An owl screeched like a banshee. Bats swooped and dived through the trees after moths. The shadowy cathedral of the day with its pillar-like tree trunks towering overhead became a vast underground vault, pitch-black except for where the breaks in the leafy canopy let in the fitful silver moonlight.

The howl came again.

'There, see! Sounds like a wolf,' she insisted.

Jake put a matey arm around her.

'Dogs, wolves, same deal. Stop worrying, nothing's going to happen.' He suddenly gave a roar and ran and rugby-tackled a boy in front and they rolled into the leaves whilst the girls screamed.

She walked on alone, her shoulders up round her ears. The wood had once been part of the great Sherwood Forest. Some of its oak trees could have witnessed the comings and goings of Robin Hood and his merry men. Romans had smelted iron there, Saxons had burned charcoal. It was far, far older than the town that had been eating at its boundaries for years. It had survived unploughed, untamed, undisturbed since time began, but it hadn't survived the roads that had cut it into fragments, nor the town planners. You only had to look at the names of the streets nearby – Chestnut Crescent, Oak Drive, the Beech and Rowan tower blocks – to realize that even this small corner of the once mighty Sherwood had been bigger not so long ago.

When she came to a patch of moonlight filtering down, she looked up and saw a black velvet sky with a full moon sailing across it, chased by a few scudding clouds. A breeze had got up as the light faded and was now brisk enough to make the trees creak and whisper.

But all the natural noises of the woods were completely overshadowed by the screams and laughter of the girls walking ahead of her, and the booming voices and bellows of the boys in a great mob bringing up the rear. Torch beams flickered in and out of the trees as the boys ran about, bursting with energy and excitement, picking up branches and having mock fights, tackling each other and throwing their victims to the ground, or chucking handfuls of leaves at the girls.

They walked towards a faint light showing through the trees and suddenly they were in a clearing. Tents were already set up round the outside and a group of boys were trying to get a fire started in a circle of stones, but were spending more time arguing and trying to burn each other with matches than getting the kindling alight. A stack of bottles and cans stood to one side. Someone had raided their garden shed for supplies and four or five long flares made from bamboo canes whose tops had been dipped and redipped in thick, coloured wax had been set up round the outside and were providing fitful yellow light.

Gwen was immediately sucked into a cluster of her friends, so Nell sat down on a log near the fire and hugged her knees, her jumper over her hands and the damp night air already trying to make her hair twist itself into corkscrews again. Suddenly a deep bass note boomed out across the clearing and rolled out over the trees. Then another. Then the drumbeat got going and the rest of the song crashed in; Jake's portable speakers were making the forest ring.

Around her the shadows danced as girls screamed and boys hollered. It was as though they'd slipped back two thousand years, now that the town was blacked out. They could've been Bronze Age Celts painted in woad who were dancing around the fire, eyeing each other up. She picked up a stick and poked it in the fire for something to do. No one else seemed to be worried about being here.

But no one else had a mind that was shouting danger over and over again. No one else had goose bumps. No one else had received a warning from a mystery boy.

That message, the big NO – was it for her? Was it a second warning? How could a boy manage to alter the lights in a whole building, just before the town blacked out? Without meaning to, she found herself scanning the darkness to see if he was out there, watching her. But there was no one.

Then, carried on the breeze, the church bells rang out nine o'clock.

Only three more hours till midnight. He'd said don't

go into the woods *tonight*. After twelve it wasn't technically night any more. It was morning. Which meant that if his warning was genuine, then she only had a few hours to wait.

The night wore on. She yawned and wrapped her coat around herself. The music flowed through the trees and was whirled high into the air by the strengthening wind. The moon still shone down, but the ragged clouds were scudding across ever faster. She watched the girls and boys dancing, hugging, kissing. Everyone looked different in firelight; Gwen looked like something from *A Midsummer Night's Dream*, her eyes luminous as she draped herself around Jake. It was certainly better than the sweet sixteen parties she'd seen on cable, where the daughters were given sports cars and had tantrums if Daddy had ordered the wrong colour.

The church clock rang for ten o'clock, its chimes fading and then getting louder as the wind eddied through the trees.

She kept watching the shadows, but she didn't see Evan River. She knew that if he came to the party, everyone would talk to him, hand him a can, and then forget he ever existed. The bees would buzz, that blank look come over their eyes, and if she asked any of them about him, they would say, oh yeah, the white-haired boy, he's cute, and then forget all about him.

Something rustled in the undergrowth behind her. The little voice began again, yelling danger over and over. She glanced into the darkness, towards the path that led to the mist.

A flash of white. A branch waving wildly as though something had gone past.

She leaped to her feet. Was it him, was it Evan?

She tiptoed to the start of the trees. There it was again – deep in the shadows, something white and low down, flitting like a ghost through the trees. She took a step forward and a twig snapped under her foot. The ghostly white blur stopped and suddenly two cold blue eyes lit up like light bulbs. They were staring straight at her.

She froze. Only animals' eyes glowed like that. For a few beats of her thumping heart they stared at each other, and then it was as though the animal blinked and turned away. She saw a flash of white again and it was gone.

That was not a Staffie. Jake was wrong. Staffies were like piano stools with a bowed leg at each corner, they barrelled along when they moved. That thing had moved like liquid. It flowed.

She began to shiver and couldn't stop. She thought she'd seen Evan with a wolf in town. OK, Jackie said it was probably a husky, and it hadn't been white, but a dark grey. Now she thought she'd seen another. She looked around to see if anyone else had noticed, but no one had. She should tell someone, but what could she say?

Hey, everyone, I saw a wolf. Oh wait, it might've been a dog. Or perhaps even a ghost dog . . .

That would give Paige and Bria something to laugh about. Hélène would've had the quick thinking to take a photo on her mobile. But at this moment she wasn't Hélène and no one would believe her. She hurried back to the fire. It seemed the only sensible thing to do. All animals hated fire, she would be safe there.

It seemed like ages before the bells rang out again, eleven chimes now.

Why was time passing so slowly? All she wanted to do was get Gwen and go home. Her sister was definitely drunk. She seemed to be arguing with Jake, although it was hard to tell because they were both staggering a bit and sometimes shouting, sometimes whispering as though their volume controls had broken. It seemed to revolve round whether Jake had gone off into the darkness with Becca.

After a while, Gwen came and squashed on to the log beside her.

'Aw, sis!' she said, when she saw Nell's worried

face. 'What's up, babe?' She took a swig from the bottle she was clutching. 'Tell me all.'

'I saw something in the shadows,' Nell said quickly. 'I think we should go. It's dangerous here tonight. I can feel it.'

'Yeah,' said Gwen vaguely.

'I know it sounds stupid, but I think there's a wolf hanging round,' she continued. 'I think it's to do with the mist. And to do with Evan. He warned me not to come into the woods. Can we go?'

'Yeah.'

The fire chose that moment to flare up and it shone on Gwen's face. Nell paused, her heart sinking.

'Actually it wasn't a wolf, it was an elephant,' she finished.

'Yeah. Elephant,' murmured Gwen. She was staring at Jake, and biting her lip. 'Do you think Jake fancies Becca? He keeps smiling at her behind my back.'

Nell gave a sigh. She'd thought for a moment that Gwen was actually worried about her and had come over to see if she was OK.

'Why would he smile at Becca when he's got you,' she soothed.

Gwen picked at the bottle label. 'I know. I used to think it worked like that. Maybe it doesn't, Nell.'

Nell had to stop her mouth dropping open. 'Hey, I'm the worried one! You're the go-getter. Go get Jake!'

Gwen looked startled, then stared over at Jake. 'You're right. I won't think like that. I'm party girl. I can't come second, ever.' She squared her shoulders, gave Nell her dazzling smile and hugged her. 'Thanks, babe.' Then she was gone.

Nell stared into the flames and let her mind wander into a daydream where she was the life and soul of the party and everyone listened to her and laughed at her jokes.

After a while someone said, 'I know, let's tell ghost stories.'

She blinked and looked around. Time must have passed. Others were sitting around the fire now. Gwen and Jake were there. So were Bria and Paige.

'I know one, I swear it's true,' said Becca. 'It happened to this mate of my mum's. Her daughter was out with her boyfriend, and their car ran out of petrol. It was about one in the morning and they were totally alone in the middle of nowhere.'

'I bet I know what they were doing!' shouted someone.

'Shush! So the boy goes for help, and tells his girlfriend to lock the doors. She sits there, waiting for her boyfriend to come back. Suddenly, something bangs on the windscreen. She looks up to see . . .' Becca paused.

'What?' breathed about three people at once.

'Oh my God, hold me!' shouted Gwen.

'. . . Not her boyfriend, but a weird madman, laughing like a lunatic. And she sees that he's swinging something in his right hand. He sticks his face close to the window and slowly pulls up his right hand. In it is her boyfriend's decapitated head . . .'

Squeals rebounded around the clearing.

'I'm gonna chuck,' said Gwen.

'Wait. Wait. There's more. So she faints and when she comes round, he's still there but he's holding something else up.'

'What?' cried Gwen.

'The car keys!'

Screams all round. 'And the moral is,' said Becca, 'don't go snogging in cars with boys.'

The girls hooted with laughter.

Urban myth, thought Nell, pulling her fur collar round her ears. It's always a friend of a friend, they're never true; but she shivered and glanced around anyway. Come on midnight, hurry up! she pleaded silently.

'Your turn,' said Gwen.

Someone nudged her. She looked up. 'Huh?'

'Your turn.'

'To do what?'

Gwen rolled her eyes. 'Space case. I said – it's your turn to tell a ghost story.'

All eyes were on her. Her mind went blank, she couldn't think of a single story. She saw Paige begin to smirk.

'I know one about the Elf-King's daughter,' she blurted out.

Bria and Paige exploded with laughter and for once she didn't blame them. Why had that story come into her mind? It wasn't an urban myth, just something her nan used to tell them, as they sat on her swing seat on the porch and shivered at the sight of the dark wood at the bottom of her garden.

'No offence,' said Paige, which meant she was definitely, one hundred per cent about to be offensive. 'But that's a fairy story. Not a ghost story.'

Nell wanted to fade into the shadows and go home right away, but then rescue came from a totally unexpected direction.

'Are you mocking my nan, Paige?' Gwen gave the girl her ice-pack stare. 'This is her story. So shut it and listen.' Then she gave her sister a big smile. 'Go Nell.'

Nell stared into the fire, to avoid the circle of eyes. 'Um, well, it's about the woods – like this one,' she said. 'It's sort of a warning about mists.'

'Like the one in the hollow,' added Gwen.

'Yeah. If you're in a wood and you see a mist that never moves, then don't step inside because it's a gateway to somewhere else.'

'Cool,' said Jake. 'I'd go straight in.'

'Get to the freaky bit,' said Gwen, impatiently. 'About the baby.'

The circle of faces grew still and quiet. Was Evan River out there, listening under the cover of darkness? She shook the thought away.

'In the olden days,' she began, 'there was this girl who lived in a house in the woods. And next to it was a patch of mist that never moved. One day she saw a stranger come out of it, and she fell in love with him.'

'Probably a dosser or a wino!' giggled Paige.

Gwen thumped the girl's arm. 'It's like talking to leaf mould! I told you to shut up,' she said. 'You can hang around us but you don't get to speak!'

'So anyway,' Nell continued, feeling ridiculous, 'the man told her he was the Elf-King and he showed her how to dance through the mist and enter his world.'

Like Evan, she thought. He'd sort of danced through the mist. Was that why the story had popped into her mind after all these years? She'd been about five years old when her nan had first told them the story. It had been a night like this, silvery and ghostly, the swing seat creaking on Dru's patio and the trees at the bottom of the garden answering back.

'When they got to his palace the girl wanted to stop there with him, but he gave her a warning. If she stayed longer than a night and a day, from sundown to sundown, then a terrible curse would befall her and she'd die. She didn't care, she was head over heels, so she stayed. For a year they were happy together, and he gave her a thousand gold necklaces and showered her with precious jewels.'

'Yum yum,' said Gwen.

'Then she had a baby girl, and the Elf-King loved his little daughter. He called her his elskling, which means precious one, in his language.'

'Elskling,' said Gwen, and looped her arms around Jake's neck.

'But she got homesick for her own world,' continued Nell, trying to stop herself looking into the shadows. 'They had this huge row about it.'

'That happened to my cousin,' said Becca. 'She and her boyfriend argued about the baby and they had to go to court.'

Everyone shushed her.

'The Elf-King reminded her about his warning,' Nell carried on. 'He said if she left now she'd die. But she thought it was just a trick to make her stop there.'

'My cousin had to go into a women's refuge,' said Becca, amidst a chorus of shushes.

'So one dark night,' said Nell, ignoring the interruption, 'she secretly packed up her things and ran back through the mist with her baby. She ran into her house and shut all the windows. Then she nailed a horseshoe over the door, because she knew that the Elf-King would hunt her down and he hated iron more than anything else in the world.'

'Here's the creepy bit,' said Gwen, hugging her knees.

'It wasn't a moment too soon. The girl heard the Elf-King howling for revenge as he ran out of the mist. He was mad with grief. She ran to draw the curtains but he was there! His chalk-white face pressed to the glass.'

No one moved. They were waiting for the finale. Nell's mind slipped back over the years, the party faded away, the log she was sitting on became the swing seat. She and Gwen were sitting huddled together, two little girls, eyes wide. Nan was in the chair opposite, one of her fairytale books on her knee, but she wasn't reading from it, she was staring at the dark wood. Nan's voice trickled into her mind.

'And the Elf-King tried to get in but the horseshoe

above the door held him back. 'My little elskling!' he howled. 'My precious baby! I can't reach her for the sting of iron.' Then he pointed a finger at the girl. 'You're cursed now,' he cried. 'I told you – stop longer than a night and day and you will die if you leave. Look at yourself in the mirror.' So she did, and she screamed in horror. Her youth and beauty had gone, she was old, her hair white, her face as wrinkled as an old apple. She staggered back and reached for an armchair, but she was dead before she sat down.'

At this point her grandmother had turned to them and said in a scary voice that made the two little girls cling together, 'That was the start of the Elf-King's curse. Every hundred years the Elven would take a human child in revenge. And they couldn't escape, because if they did, they would age and die.'

Nell sat back. The swing seat faded. The crackle of the fire came back. Gwen was staring at her from the other side of the fire, her arms around Jake. The times when she and Gwen sat huddled together were long over. Everyone else was staring too, their faces lit by the fire.

'The end,' she added, to make sure they realized the story was over.

'That is so stupid, how can you age in one night!' said Paige, breaking the silence.

'It could happen,' said Jake. 'Maybe time runs differently in each world. Or the atmosphere poisons humans if they stay too long.'

'Anyway, it is stupid,' added Bria, scornfully. 'How can you be allergic to iron?'

'You can,' said Nell. 'I know someone who is.'

Was that another reason why the story had leaped into her mind? Evan had two things in common with the Elf-King. Her eyes flicked towards the dark circle of trees around them, but she could see nothing moving, not even the ghostly white dog.

'Anyone know a proper ghost story?' said Paige spitefully.

But no one seemed to be in the mood any more. Some were heading for the tents, some began searching round for something to eat. A couple of boys began building the fire up.

And then the church bells rang out for midnight. Nell counted the chimes, *six*, *seven*, *eight* . . .

She began to relax. Nothing had happened. Evan was talking big – trying to scare her, that's all.

Nine, *ten*, *eleven* . . .

And the wolf was probably a big dog, a blue-eyed Alsatian.

Twelve.

Yes! Tension unwound inside her like a rubber band. The night had ended, that meant she was safe – didn't it?

As the echoes of the last chime died away, Jake staggered into the middle of the clearing.

'Hey. Anyone seen Gwen?'

Seven

Nell ran through the trees. She'd tugged one of the flares out of the ground, and she was holding it in front of her, the flame guttering and smoking and throwing weird shadows everywhere.

'Gwen! Where are you?' she called. 'Just answer me!'

She moved from one patch of moonlight to the next, the hairs on the back of her neck standing on end, as though a part of her knew that something ancient and alien was watching her. She had no idea which way Gwen might have gone, but her feet seemed to want to go towards the mist, so she headed that way.

As she felt the ground start to slope downwards she thought she saw something move in the darkness. There was no moonlight now, the clouds were covering it completely. She heard a low growl.

'Gwen,' she whispered, with a tremble in her voice.

'Stay still, if you can hear me.'

She held the torch higher and the billowing yellow light streamed out and lit the scene before her.

Her heart nearly stopped.

It looked like a beautiful oil painting called *Terrified Girl and Wolf by Torchlight*.

Gwen was backed against a tree trunk. Her face was hysterical, her eyes diamond-shaped and glittering with tears. Her handbag was lying at her feet, but her make-up, hairbrush, purse and perfume spray were scattered across the grass as though she'd been swinging it wildly.

The wolf had her cornered. It was a metre away, its eyes like sapphires in the flarelight, its arctic-white coat luminous. A twig snapped under Nell's foot. The merciless eyes turned to her, dismissed her, then pinned Gwen again.

'Nell!' she sobbed. 'Do something!'

Nell had no chance. The wolf sprang. It reared up, furious and savage, its gaping jaws reaching for Gwen's throat. Gwen made a gasping noise, small but terrible, and fell back against the tree trunk.

Without thinking, Nell dropped the flare and ran forward. She grabbed Gwen's perfume spray, dropped it, fumbled, picked it up again, aimed and pressed the button. There was a hiss and a choking stream of flowery scent went straight into the wolf's eyes and nose.

It went berserk. It turned on her, savage and furious. Its blood-covered muzzle concertinaed back, its eyes became slits. Something glinted in its jaws. It was Gwen's birthday necklace. The wolf had torn it from her throat. It spat it out and then sprang towards Nell. She fell back, her hand landing near the flare. It was still burning. She grabbed it and swiped it through the air, leaving golden trails. The wolf gave a maddened snarl and snatched at it.

'Thor!' growled a deep voice.

The wolf froze. Nell scrambled to her feet, holding the torch high.

'Who's there? Who are you?'

A tall shadow moved in the flickering yellow light. She caught a glimpse of a sleeve, a hand, locks of silvery hair blowing gently. Someone was there. Not Evan, he was too tall, but someone with the same white hair.

'I'm calling the police,' she said, backing away.

The man's voice hissed another command, in a language she didn't know. The wolf gave her one last icy glare and then it turned and faded into the dark after the figure.

Nell hurried towards her sister. 'Quick, let's get out of here!'

Gwen was still leaning against the tree, her eyes glazed. As Nell grabbed her arm, she slowly sank to her knees and then collapsed on to the damp grass.

Nell stabbed the flare into the ground so that the flames lit Gwen's face, and knelt beside her.

'Stop messing around, let's go! There's a weirdo hanging around.'

Gwen lay where she'd fallen with her eyes half closed and her eyebrows drawn down as if still puzzled about something.

Nell pushed her sister's hair back out of her face. Her fingers turned sticky. She held them towards the light of the flare. They were scarlet. Gwen was bleeding! She pulled the flare closer. There were bite marks on her neck and one long cut where the wolf had dragged the necklace from her. Blood was dripping down on to the grass.

'Please, Gwen, can you walk? We have to get you some help.'

Gwen lay still. Nell rocked back on her heels. She couldn't leave her, not like this! But help was coming, she could hear voices shouting close by. One was Jake's, calling out for Gwen as he searched along the paths. She breathed a sigh of relief.

'Gwen, I'm going to get help. I'll be a few seconds.'

She turned and ran, her heart thundering, her breath sobbing, until a moment later she ran straight into Jake.

He stumbled about in a drunken way. 'You found her?' he slurred.

'Come with me. Something's happened!' She grabbed his arm.

'Has she been sick? I told her cider was a no-no.'

'She's bleeding, Jake. She's been attacked.'

She dragged him back to where Gwen had fallen, Jake pointing the flashlight of his mobile.

No Gwen!

The flare was still there. So were her handbag and the dark stains of blood on the grass. The broken necklace was there too. She picked it up. It smelled of Gwen's perfume. But Gwen had gone. She looked around wildly. She'd only been away for a few moments.

'Where is she?' said Jake, sobering up quickly.

'She was here. Unconscious,' she cried.

Something rustled in the bushes behind her. She pushed the necklace into her pocket and whirled round. Footsteps moved away at high speed. She began to run, her feet slipping as she hit the slope of the hollow. Below her the mist writhed like white paint in water. And for a moment she thought she saw a tall figure carrying something in his arms and the silhouette of the wolf at his feet. They were fleeing into the mist.

She careered madly down the slope after them, not thinking just reacting. Her feet skidded and slid on the stepping stones, brambles tore at her, but she came to the other side without seeing anything more. No shadowy figure. No wolf. No sister.

Her breath sobbing, she ran back to Jake. 'I-I-I saw this man in the shadows. I think he took her into the mist'

Jake grabbed her. 'You saw a stranger and you left her here alone?'

'I heard you shout. You were close. It was a few seconds.'

'Chrissake, Nell!'

A torch beam flickered. 'What's happening,' said Becca, running down the path to them. 'Where's Gwen?'

Nell took a deep breath. 'She's gone, and I saw this stranger hanging about. He had a creature with him. It went for Gwen and now there's this.' She sank to her knees and held the flare so that the blood shone like rubies.

'Oh my God!' wailed Becca and ran back to the clearing.

'We – we need to call the police,' said Jake, and sat down with a thump, the way a toddler sits, straight down on to his bottom. A couple of minutes later more torches began to weave their way through the trees.

Soon after that the screaming started.

Eight

Nell heard the sirens wailing into life from all parts of the town as the call went out that there'd been an incident in the wood.

Police cars were on the way, and a paramedic, but there would be nothing for him to do, except treat Gwen's hysterical friends. Nell willed the cars to get there faster. They'd already been beaten by other kids from Woodbridge Road and the estate next to it, drawn by a spreading network of text messages. Girls were huddled in groups sobbing. Others were morbidly videoing the blood, until Gwen's friends came along and snatched their mobiles and threw them into the bushes. The crime scene was being trampled. Some of the more practical partygoers were trying to hide the pile of empty cans, shoving them in backpacks, handing them to some of the newcomers, telling them to dump them in the nearest bin.

She crouched on her own and wished this moment to be over. She wanted *now* to run away as fast it could and become *then*.

Would anyone believe her when she told them what she saw? Would even her mother believe her? *There was a wolf and the shadow of a man, honest. And they took Gwen into the mist.* Why couldn't this have been another example of her pathetic obsessive urge to worry about things that didn't happen? Why did her worry about the party have to come true? Why couldn't this be Gwen doing her usual attention-seeking routine, wandering off so that she could make a big scene later.

Why didn't the police get here? Why didn't her mum come and tell her it was going to be all right?

Then someone gave a relieved shout and flashlights began to show up between the trees as some of the kids led the police and the paramedic towards them. From then on it was noise and movement, police radios burbling, voices shouting, orders given.

'See, this is her phone! And this is her blood!'

'Get back, all of you! Stop trampling about.'

'What the hell has been going on here? Someone been having a party?'

'You older ones, get everyone over there.'

'Who's gone missing?'

For a moment the babble of voices went quiet.

'Gwen Church,' said Nell.

The silence held.

'Bloody hell,' said a voice in the darkness. Then more quietly: 'Has someone told Jackie.'

The officers began whispering to each other. One of them made a call.

'She's on her way here now. I'll go and get her,' he said and headed off towards the entrance.

A policewoman put her arm around Nell, saying, 'You'll see, this will be OK. Your mum'll be here soon.'

'I saw someone,' she said, but the policewoman had gone.

Around her the police who'd arrived first were rounding up the partygoers and taking names and addresses, which was hard work because many of them were hysterical, the girls sobbing, the boys trying to make out that they hadn't had that much to drink. Half of them were giving false names or slinking off through the trees. Jake was sitting on the log by the fire, his elbows on his knees, his head bowed, whilst a policewoman sat with her arm around him, talking softly.

A giant hand seemed to be squeezing all the air out of Nell's lungs, she could hardly breath. A shadow flitted over to her, a torch beam bobbing madly, and then she was being enveloped in a fierce hug. It was Jackie, in uniform, smelling of ozone and car exhaust and the vinegary chips she'd had for her dinner.

'You're safe!' she exclaimed. 'But where's Gwen? They said someone was missing. Not Gwen. No, not Gwen!'

'Sorry, Mum!' she said. 'Sorry. Sorry.' It was all she could think of to say.

Jackie took her by the shoulders. She could feel her mother's fingernails digging through the fur coat. 'How much did she drink?'

'I don't know,' said Nell.

'You know what she's like — has she run off with another boy? To make Jake jealous or something?'

'No! I saw something, Mum. There was this man nearby. I saw his shadow.'

Jackie shook her. 'What? You should've rung me. You should have told me about the party.'

'Sorry!' She took a deep breath. 'The shadow I saw, I think some people live in the mist. You know, like the boy I told you about at school.'

'What boy?'

'I told you this morning!'

'Oh, don't go on about that now, Nell.'

'He lives in the mist.'

Jackie stared at her. 'What?'

Nell clutched her mother's sleeve. 'There must be another path that leads to somewhere else . . .'

Jackie frowned at her and removed her clutching hand. 'Nell, have you been drinking?'

'No!'

'Then just go and calm down. Please. You know how you get. I have to help with the search.'

Jackie looked round wildly. Parents were turning up from every direction, calling for their sons and daughters, hugging them, pulling them away, or talking sheepishly to the police. Most of the kids at the party had houses that backed on to the woods like hers. Nell could see the relief in the adults' eyes as they realized that their child wasn't the one who'd walked into the shadows and not come out again. Jackie dragged her over to one of the policemen.

'He'll take you back to the station, soon. Won't you, Bob?'

Bob turned round and put a big hand on her shoulder. 'Oh God, Jackie, yes of course, anything. Then I'll be back to search. Don't worry, we'll find her.'

Jackie shook her head helplessly. 'Nell,' she said. 'I have to go.'

Nell nodded and pushed her. 'Sorry. Sorry. Go!'

She watched her mother walk away. 'Church,' she was saying into her phone. 'Get to the woods. Now!'

The wood became full of shouts and whistles and the burble of radios, as the police spread out and searched it. The white beams of their torches flickered and strobed through the trees.

In the clearing there were forensics teams, and a couple of dog-handlers with German Shepherds straining at their leashes. Others were putting up crime-scene tape and beyond that Nell could see huddles of kids sobbing and hugging each other.

She waited until her mother had disappeared, waited quietly until Bob turned back and began taking down some more names and addresses. Then she ran. Not to her home, but to the mist.

Away from the clearing, the woods closed around her as though she'd gone blind. The strengthening wind was beating clouds over the face of the moon and the air had become cold and damp. Rays of silver light still shone down through the trees every now and then. They didn't look fairytale any more, they looked threatening.

She tripped and fumbled her way along the path towards the hollow again, wishing she'd thought to grab a torch.

I have to do this, for Gwen, she thought, digging her

nails into her palms to take her mind off the fear that threatened to engulf her.

She stumbled her way towards the hollow, jumping at every creak and rustle, the white wolf haunting her mind. At last she reached it. The mist was glowing like neon. She began to slide down towards it, the scent of pine needles swirling around her.

'You wait till Church hears,' said a voice very loudly, close behind her.

She glanced back and saw two police officers she vaguely knew, one male, one female. Jackie must have sent them to check out the hollow and the mist.

She scurried behind a bush and kept very still.

'He'll go ballistic,' the woman continued. 'His own daughter spending the night in the woods, getting drunk.'

'She's a right little madam, that Gwen.'

Nell clenched her fists. Stop talking about her like that, she ordered silently. She crouched down as they came by her, their torch beams lancing through the darkness.

'I wouldn't let my daughter's boyfriend spend the evening in her bedroom, door closed.'

'The other one, Nell, she's an odd little thing. Everyone thinks she's mousy but she's got a sarky tongue, always peering out from under her hair, watching everything.'

'Scared of her own shadow, though. She says she saw a stranger hanging about.'

'Thirteen years old and she's out in the woods at midnight – what's Jackie thinking!'

'There's something fishy going on, I reckon. I mean, maybe Gwen met someone on the internet, and she's run off with him? She doesn't look the sort to pick her relationships carefully.'

'God help whoever took her when Church gets hold of him. He even scares me when he goes off on one,' said the policewoman.

Nell sat back on her heels. So her dad inspired fear in everyone, not just her.

The two officers walked by, their torch beams scanning the bushes and trees either side. They went down the slope, never noticing her, and at the bottom they began cursing and then jumping from stone to stone, the policeman complaining that his foot had gone ankle deep in mud when he slipped. For a few steps their torches lit the mist from within, then she heard them start up the slope on the other side.

She waited until their voices had faded, then she walked down to the stepping stones. They were made of some kind of white stone that contained quartz flecks that glowed in the moonlight. They marched ahead of her until the thick mist blotted them out. It blotted out sounds too. The babble of the police radios, the voices of the parents and the sobbing girls went quiet. The heavenly music was there, though. This time there was the faintest murmur of voices too. She clutched her hands together to stop them shaking, the cuffs of her fur coat sticky with Gwen's blood. It was as though there were people near her but she couldn't see them.

She hesitated with her foot on the first stone.

Here she was again, on the edge of things. She was drawn to them, she always sat at the edge of the class, always at the edge of any group. Now this – somehow it felt like the edge of the world.

She was about to break every sensible precaution for staying safe. Someone like Hélène Beauchamp would not be in this mess, Hélènes never were. They would have a plan, they would never have let it happen in the first place. But she was Nell, and it had happened. Nothing's safe whatever we do, she thought. The worst has happened to Gwen. Now I have to do something, take control of this terrible thing.

Her nan's story said that the way into the other place was to dance over the stones. She stared at them, replaying in her mind the image of Evan hopping and skipping in front of her, when she'd first followed him.

She took a deep breath. Her heart began beating so loudly that she had to tap her chest so she wouldn't feel it any more. She jumped on to the next stone, the mist settling around her. She made herself remember Evan's moves. One step forward, two to the side, one forward, one to the other side. Her hair caught on twigs and brambles, nearly scalping her, but she pulled it loose each time and carried on.

She kept going for the first ten steps, blinded by the mist, her feet moving in the rhythm, then she began to shake and her knees went weak, because with each step a terrible fear had come over her – she felt as though she was high above the earth and the next step would see her plunge to her death. Vertigo gripped her in its dizzying grasp.

It's some sort of trick, she told herself desperately. It's to make people turn back. She had to ignore it. She felt around for the next stone. Her blood ran cold – there was nothing below her reaching foot, she would fall into an abyss and her parents would lose both of their children.

No. She could do this. She couldn't see forward or backward, so the only thing to do was to keep going. To start with the mist had clung to her face like wet tissue. Now it was getting thicker, it felt like hands softly sweeping across her face. A few steps further, it had the horrible texture of spider webs, and one of her horrors was walking through a web and getting it stuck in her hair and face.

But she kept dancing, fifty stones – sixty stones, she knew for a fact that there were only about twenty stepping stones before the land rose again on the other side of the hollow. But here she was, seventy steps in, and the ground was still level. The brambles had disappeared as well, only mist surrounded her now. Either the hollow had got a lot bigger or the stepping stones had led her somewhere else.

She had no idea what she was moving through. It wasn't air, land or water. She felt like she was pushing through a jellyfish.

She began to hear the music more clearly. She took one last step and her foot touched dry land. The mist swept back from her face, leaving it sticky but drying quickly. It was like stepping off an aeroplane in a foreign country. The smells and noises and the feel of the air were strange.

The last shred of the mist swirled and drew back, and she saw where she was. She was very, very far from home.

Nine

The music played on, but it seemed to be coming from everywhere, drifting over the trees that stretched before her. Rippling notes going up and down the scale, the sort of music she imagined would be played in heaven. But this wasn't heaven.

This wasn't the usual wood, either, the one with the warden that lapped the bottom of her garden. This one was much darker, wilder, the trees warped and massive. They were pine and fir, dark green, spiky-needled. They rose around her, their lowest branches disappearing into the sky, their trunks covered in lichen and mosses, and dripping with ferns. The paths that led through them were like tunnels in the undergrowth.

I shouldn't be here, she thought. This is wrong.

A lantern had been hung from one of the branches, giving a soft, yellow light. It was swaying in a breeze that smelled of pine. Above the trees there were stars, but they seemed to be folded over each other as though the sky had been twisted.

Nothing was right here.

Something howled deep inside the rustling, creaking darkness, and was answered by another. Wolves. No mistake this time. She wanted to run back through the mist to safety, but she couldn't. She bent down and picked up something from the grass. It was an earring.

Gwen was here somewhere.

And not only Gwen. Movements fluttered in the corner of her eye. She whirled around. There were others out there, flitting amongst the trees. By the swaying light of the lantern she could see charcoal eyes full of trickiness staring at her. The light caught their white hair and turned it to silver, and sparkled on the gold at their throats and ears.

'Wait,' she said, trying to follow their movements. She was pretty sure they were kids. 'You've got to help me . . .' But there was a shiver of movement in the darkness and they were gone, dissolving like ghosts.

That didn't matter any more because now Evan was walking towards her.

He came out from between the trees, the light striping on his face, half light, half dark, so that he looked as though he was wearing war paint. Around his feet fawned the skinny, leggy grey wolf she'd seen him with outside the jeweller's. Something was wrong with one of its back legs, making it hop like a bunny. When he stopped in front of her it stopped too, as though it was a trained dog, and then curled at his feet.

'Where is she?' She thumped him hard in the chest with both her hands. He moved back. He didn't do anything to protect himself. He didn't say anything. He watched her from under his spiky fringe.

'Where is she?'

Something moved in the trees. The others were still out there, watching. Maybe they'd rush in and do a Rikstall, ten against one. She didn't care. Adrenaline coursed through her blood. She just wanted Gwen back.

She thumped him again, fear and anger boiling over. 'Come on – tell me!'

This time his hands moved super-fast and caught hers.

'Stop,' he said, as the wolf stood up ominously, and a low growl echoed from its throat. 'I don't fight girls.'

She tried to pull her hands away, but she couldn't budge from his grasp. A tear hovered on her lower eyelashes. She blinked it away; she wouldn't let him see her crying. She wasn't Gwen, tears weren't one of her weapons.

'You tell me right now, Evan,' she said, her voice choked. 'What's going on?'

He ignored her question. 'How did you do that – how did you get through the mist?'

'When my sister disappears, I learn quickly.'

He shook his head. 'You saw me cross the stones once and you remembered,' he said. 'That's so clever.'

'I remember everything. It's like a curse sometimes.'

'It's got you in trouble this time.'

She could hardly get her breath. 'I don't care.'

'Can I let you go?' he said. 'Only Faolan was getting antsy because you were hitting me.'

'Faolan?'

'My wolf.'

She looked down into the wolf's amber eyes. They weren't friendly.

'It means little she-wolf in the old language,' he said.

Faolan stared some more, then she yawned hugely, showing off an impressive and scary set of fangs. Nell got the message.

'OK, I'll stop,' she said quickly.

The grip on her hands released and he let go. She stuck her hands in the pockets of her fur coat and took a few deep breaths, making herself calm down.

'There was another wolf. It bit Gwen,' she said. 'Not

this one. It was white. And there was a guy, older than you, taller.'

'Fen and his wolf, Thor. It didn't hurt her too badly,' Evan said quickly. 'It was trying to take the necklace off. She'll be healed.'

As if it knew it was being talked about, a wolf howled deep in the forest.

'You have to go back now,' he said urgently.

She didn't move. 'I don't even know where I am.'

'In the woods.'

'Not the woods I recognize,' she said.

'This is our land.'

'I don't understand.'

He gave a ghost version of his normal grin. 'Nor does Google Earth, it really screws up round here,' he said. 'It can't handle mists that lead to other places . . .'

It was her turn to shake her head. 'No, it can't be true. It's impossible,' she stammered.

Whilst Hélène whispered, then why're the hairs on your arm sticking up, and why're your teeth chattering? Something's very very wrong, and you know it. You're way out of your depth here.

'I want my sister back and then I'll go,' she said. 'She'll be hysterical. She hates nature, let alone wild animals!'

There was not even the ghost of a smile on Evan's face now.

'I warned you, but you didn't listen. She's ours now,' he said.

Nell stared at him. 'What?'

'You don't walk in here and get her back.'

'You can't do that,' she said.

'We can.' He stared at her as if she was a stranger. She might never have sat and eaten lunch with him, or saved him from Rikstall's gang. 'We might look like you, but we aren't. And we don't think like you, either.'

'So who are you?' she said, her hand going to her throat as if she were trying to strangle herself.

He shrugged a shoulder, as if what he was about to say was no big deal. 'We're your ancient enemy, Nell. We're the Elven.'

The trees rustled in the light breeze. Amongst them there was a glint of sharp metal, as though someone carried a weapon. Whispers blew about. The others were still out there, listening and watching. So was Faolan. The wolf's eyes never left Nell. The lantern swayed, sending shadows chasing everywhere, especially across Evan's face.

'Ever wondered why fairytales are so bloody?' he said. 'Because they're the record of a battle. It's been

going on for centuries. Elven against human, human against Elven.'

'No,' said Nell. 'They're just stories my nan tells. Elves aren't real.'

'Elven,' he corrected. 'Not elves, or elvish or Elfin.'

She waved her hands as though batting his words away. 'No. This can't be true.'

'Yes, it can. We shared the world with you – until you forced us out. Believe me, Nell, a thousand years ago you loved us. We were the princes and princesses of the forests,' he said. 'Then everything changed. Suddenly there were lots more humans and not many Elven. You got scared of us. We didn't obey the rules. We danced in the moonlight and hid in the woods. We had powers.'

'Yes,' she said, clinging to something she knew to be true. 'You can make people forget about you.'

'Like this.' He looked thoughtful for a moment and then the sound of bees floated around him. It was like watching a cat purring – the noise was there but you couldn't tell how it was being made. And somehow it made you relax. 'We call it charm. We use it to alter the frequency of your mind, so that you forget.'

'Not me.'

He nodded in acknowledgement. 'Yes, you're special.'

'So how come you got pushed out of the world?' she

said. 'You're more powerful than us.'

He wrinkled his nose and, without thinking, rubbed the scar across his palm from the fight with Rikstall. 'You learned our weaknesses.'

'Iron?'

'Yes. It hurts so much, Nell. It burns like ice, it turns our bones to paste, it makes our teeth ache and blinds our eyes. It's terrible, it even makes our *hair* ache. And it scatters our thoughts so that we can't charm you and make you forget. We can't even think straight – imagine having the worst headache in your life and then having to sit a maths test.'

Deep in the pocket of her fur coat, her fingers found Gwen's broken necklace and squeezed it tight.

'You're not a fairytale,' she said, slowly.

He nodded. 'A long time ago you wiped us from your history, *you* made us into fairytales. Suits us most of the time. We see you, you don't see us. And even though you took the world from us . . .' he waved a hand around at the forest, '. . . five hundred years ago we stole a part of it back, and made it ours.'

'You can't steal land.'

'You can when you have powerful devices. They can take a forest and twist it into another dimension. And hide gateways to your world in the mist, so we can come to

94

you, but you can't come to us.'

'What has this to do with me?'

Suddenly he was looking everywhere but at her. He kicked at a stone. 'Now things have changed.'

'How?' said Nell.

He stared over her shoulder as though suddenly fascinated by the trees. 'We want our world back.'

Ice ran down her spine. 'It's not yours.'

'It's not yours, either.' He met her eyes. 'But that doesn't stop the Watchers imprisoning us.'

'Who?' said Nell.

'They're humans who are immune to our charm, like you. They police the Elven, and arrest us if we're caught in your world.'

'You've been into our school. You didn't get caught.'

'I was lucky. If I'd been caught by a Watcher I would have been sent to the iron camps.'

'What're they?' she said, although by the look on his face, they weren't holiday parks.

'Prisons far to the north,' he said bitterly. 'Thousands of miles away from anywhere. The fences around them are twenty feet high and made of iron. All the Elven inside are weak, they can't even think straight.'

Wolves howled in the forest again, but closer this time. He listened for a moment and then quickly reached up and took the lantern from the trees and beckoned her to follow him. He was leading her back to the mist, she could see it glowing white through the trees.

'No.' She stopped. 'I'm not going back till I get Gwen.'

'Yes, you are.' He made a small sign to Faolan and suddenly the wolf was hopping over, her lips curled, showing her fangs. The look in her amber eyes said that she was going to enjoy this. Nell quickly began to walk. The wolf followed, her nose almost touching the back of Nell's knees, growling softly.

'My mother and father are in one of those iron camps,' Evan said, when Nell had caught up. 'They made the mistake of coming into your world and getting arrested.' He patted Faolan, who gave Nell a very smug look.

'You have to live on your own?' she said, following him but keeping her distance from the wolf.

'There's more of us.'

She knew that. A girl dressed all in white with long, long hair in cornrow plaits was flitting along behind them, keeping well back so that she was only a ghostly shape. The Elven were making sure she left their land.

'But no adults, they've all gone to the camps,' Evan continued. 'We have a palace deep in the forest. It's OK, though, our mamas taught us to survive, to stand up for ourselves.'

She grabbed his arm to stop him. 'So what has this got to do with my sister?' she demanded.

He shrugged her hand away. 'The curse, Nell. Don't you remember the story you told everyone an hour ago?'

So he had been watching her! She shivered. He'd been out in the darkness and she hadn't known, but she wouldn't let him see that she was bothered.

'That was a fairy story,' she said. 'It's not real.'

His eyes glinted. 'It is. It happened a long time ago – the Elf-King lost his child. The Elven have long memories.'

'You took my sister because of some stupid curse about a custody battle over a baby? That's crazy.'

'Not just the baby. The curse stands for everything else we lost to the humans. So every hundred years we take a human girl for keeps.'

Her breath caught in her throat. 'You're taking Gwen for ever?'

He didn't look anything like a schoolboy any more. He looked dangerous. 'Yes. But this time there's a twist. This time we might give her back.'

This was serious. She really couldn't stop shivering now.

The mist was thick around them, brushing its jellyfish tentacles across their faces, and sprinkling them with icy dew. She could feel her straightened hair curling itself into corkscrews again. Evan was close in front of her but it was as though there was a silk curtain between them. He looked like a ghost.

'My brother's name is Fen.' Evan held out his wrist with the small tattoo of the wolf's head. The mist dripped from his skin. 'Everyone calls him the wolf. He's a freedom fighter for our cause, the only one left. This is his plan.'

'He kidnapped Gwen. He had no right,' she said.

'He had no choice, he had to do this.'

'Really?' Her face became scornful. 'He's got compulsive kidnap disorder?'

'No.' His voice was cold. There was no laughing at her jokes now. 'When our parents got taken he swore that he would get them released. He lives to avenge them.'

'That's not Gwen's fault. I'll get her back. You tell him.'

Evan shook his head. 'He's taken her to the palace.'

They stared at each other.

'Fen's wrong,' she said. 'This is a stupid plan.'

'You don't know anything. Take it from me, he's amazing. He's our only hope.'

His hand reached out and took hers. 'Come on.' He pulled her along the white stepping stones. 'You have to leave.'

She began leaping from stone to stone. 'So why did you warn me?'

That stopped him in his tracks. 'A crazy moment. Because when I was watching you at school, you looked so . . .' He wiped the damp hair from his eyes and he looked less wild and more like the Evan she thought she knew. 'I do things sometimes. Good and bad. It's best not to trust me.'

Then he was off again, dragging her from stone to stone. The mist began to thin and become more like shreds of wet tissue paper blowing around her. She was close to her world again. She could smell exhaust fumes and the smoke from the campfire.

As the mist thinned even more and the sound of voices shouting drifted to them, he stopped and turned to her.

He took a crumpled envelope from his pocket and stared at it for a moment. Nell could see odd, angular writing on the front. 'You can save me the bother of delivering this. They'll have to take it seriously now it's coming from you.'

'Take what seriously?' she said.

He held the envelope out but she didn't take it. 'The Watchers have from now until sundown to open the iron camps. And then set the Elven free.' He paused. 'Or your sister will become ours for ever.'

Nell stepped back, her foot half sinking in the marshy ground.

'No,' she said fiercely. 'She'll be rescued. However long it takes, my mum will see to that. You won't keep her.'

From a long way away the church bells of her world rang out.

'Time's ticking, Nell,' he said. 'Dawn's nearly here. You've got till the sun goes down today. If Gwen goes back through the mist after that, then a hundred years will hit her as soon as she sets foot in your wood. She'll be old and withered before she's even lived.'

A series of pictures scrolled before Nell's horrified eyes. Gwen white-haired. Gwen bent double, crippled with arthritis. Her life over. No longer Queen Bee of her gang. No more alpha girl. No more parties in the woods. She'd go crazy! She'd probably crumble into dust at the sheer outrage.

'How can I give the letter to the Watchers?' she cried. 'I don't know any.'

'Yes, you do. You're related to one. That's why we took Gwen.'

'Who?'

He thrust the envelope in her hands. She looked down at it, and there it was, the one word in the strange square writing – Church. Nell's heart turned to stone, just seeing his name. But it figured. Her father was an expert at annoying people, so why should she be surprised that he'd managed to annoy a whole species.

'See that Church and no one else gets the message. We're not bluffing, Nell. I'll come back to the woods every hour – each time the church clock strikes. Tell them to come with proof that they've opened the camps.'

Their eyes met. His looked cool and unconcerned, his hand now resting on Faolan's head.

'But warn them, Nell, not a moment after sunset – or Gwen is ours.'

'I'll never forgive you for this,' she said.

He shrugged. 'So? Elven and human can never be friends.'

Then he and the wolf were gone.

A Warning to All Young People

Beware the Elven, my children. Do not be fooled by them. They are as beautiful as starlight, as fierce as wolves, and as heartless as ice.

They appear out of the mists, laughing and dancing their way into our villages, making our poor, dull, human lives exciting. Then we wake up next day to find our food mysteriously vanished. But worse than that, is when they sing in the night and call to us and take our daughters.

Do not listen to their singing, it will charm you and you will be lost.

Beware the Elven, we say, they live to hurt us and steal from us. It amuses them like a baby is entertained by a rattle.

More Eerie Folk Tales
By Druscilla Church, British Folklore Society

Ten

The dawn sky was the colour of washed-out ink. Long, skinny lines of pink clouds hung over a huge transparent moon that was fading as the light grew.

Tracker dogs barked, some close by, some at a distance. The trees were dripping with dew, and a mist that had nothing to do with the stuff in the hollow was wreathing the roots of the trees like low-level smoke.

Nell walked towards the clearing.

To one side a dark figure was swinging a torch from side to side so that its bright beam scythed across the ground like a light sabre. She knew what he was doing. He was forensics, and he was searching for little spatters of blood with the special blue tracker torch. Its beam was designed to light up the red blood so it shone like neon. He was wasting his time. Even if the drops led right into the mist, and there was a huge flashing sign saying *We*

Took Gwen This Way, they would still not believe it and they would still never find her.

They could draft in a thousand police officers and none of it would save her sister. She'd been stolen away into a world that couldn't be detected by clever torches that showed up blood splatter. Or by collecting tiny strands of hair or thread. Or by the officers crawling along in a line doing a fingertip search along the paths. They would find plenty of discarded things in the woods – bottles, old newspapers, schoolbooks, discarded wallets that thugs like Rikstall had stolen and emptied of money and cards. But there would be nothing that would point them towards a place that didn't exist.

Someone was shouting her mother's name. Footsteps sounded nearby. She flattened herself against a tree trunk as Jackie hurried through the trees.

'Jack! The media are here,' someone shouted. 'They want you or Church in the clearing.'

She held her breath as her mum strode past, trying to scrape her untidy hair back and straighten her uniform, her hands moving automatically.

Seeing anyone in distress was scary, but when it was a police officer, it was super-scary. These were people who sorted out traffic accidents, murder scenes, brawls; who knocked on doors and told people tragic news; who

106

trapped serial killers into confessing and talked desperate people down from bridges. So seeing her mother now, with her eyes full of panic, was the worst thing Nell had ever witnessed.

'Where's Church?' she was shouting. 'Tell him I'll deal with it.'

Then in a quieter voice, Nell heard her say to Bob, who was hurrying after her, 'If he blimmin' well says one more time that I shouldn't have let her go to the party, I'll go for him, I swear.' She grabbed Bob's arm. 'If you see him, tell him to keep looking for Nell, she's here somewhere. She's his daughter as well . . .'

They disappeared into the half-light and Nell took a few breaths and then went looking for Church. She found his car first, big and shiny and parked messily so that he was taking up a couple of spaces by the entrance to the wood. No one would tell him to shift it. Then she heard his voice booming across the woods. He was heading her way.

She perched on the bonnet and watched him come striding towards her, the early morning mist curling round his ankles. She'd been watching him all her life. Through the banisters of the stairs, when she'd make excuses not to go out on treats with Gwen and him. Through the window of his car when he'd taken them on the odd day trip and she'd refused to get out, saying she was feeling travel sick. Not that he noticed. He'd be working, talking on his phone, bored by them and twitchy to be off fighting crime again.

When he saw her he stopped dead. He gave her his Rottweiler look, all intense brown eyes that pinned people and never let go, even when he was saying something ordinary like, hello.

'Twigs. We've got half the force looking for you. Not funny.' he shouted.

He called her Twigs because she'd always been thin. She was convinced he did it out of cruelty, mocking her for not being the strapping son he would have preferred or beautiful like Gwen. 'You were supposed to stay with Bob.'

'I've got to talk to you, Dad.'

He bipped his car, threw the door open and pushed her inside. It smelled of leather and his aftershave. It also smelled new. Maybe if he didn't buy new cars, then getting money out of him for school trips or the odd lavish Christmas present wouldn't wipe the smile off Jackie's face, and make her disappear into the garden with the phone, to give him a mouthful about how much it cost to raise two daughters.

He dropped into the seat next to her, setting the car

rocking. He never did anything quietly or gently, that's why he frayed her nerves.

'Pine needles! Is that reek coming from you?' he accused, sniffing the air and wincing.

'Yes,' she said, an image of those dark trees rushing into her mind.

'Hate that smell!' He smacked the dashboard with his fist. 'But never mind. I need to know exactly what happened last night.' He turned to her. 'Some of the kids said you saw something.'

She took a deep breath. 'Dad.' She met his eyes for the first time ever. 'I know what you are.'

He stared at her. 'Of course you do,' he said, frowning. 'A detective. And now I'm going to find out who did this and make them pay.' He thumped the steering wheel this time. 'Spit it out, Twigs, what did you see?'

She tried again. 'I mean I know who you *really* are, Dad. I know about the Elven, the Watchers. You.'

His frown deepened. 'What?'

The look on her father's face was not promising, but she ploughed on. 'Evan and his brother targeted me and Gwen at school, I see that now. We used to hang around together at lunch.'

Church stared like an owl.

'And you know what Evan did?' Even now all she

wanted to do was talk about him. 'He made the lights go out as I walked along the alley. And—'

'Wait!' Church slapped a hand down on the dashboard. ' Are you saying you know two boys did this, but you've not told—'

'Not boys, Dad. Elven. I know about them. I can see them like you can.'

She stopped. Her father had begun rubbing his right earlobe. He always did that when he was angry. When she was little, whenever she saw him rub his ear, she'd scarper.

'Is this a joke?' he said.

A cold feeling began in her stomach. 'No.'

Church rubbed his ear some more. Then he shook his head slowly. 'Stop it. Right now. This is not funny.'

The cold had spread to her face, she felt herself go pale. 'It's true, you know it is. There really are Elven, like in the stories Nan tells. Evan told me you were a Watcher,' she said desperately. 'He said tell Church—'

She stopped. Something was very wrong.

Father and daughter stared at each other for far too long. Then Church sighed and sat back, his face in his hands. Nell knew that gesture. He was trying to take the irritated look off his face before he faced her. He was trying to keep his temper with her. He didn't succeed.

'Look,' he said. 'Stop making stuff up. I haven't got time. Yes, Gwen is a difficult sister to follow. I get that she's bullied you since birth and overshadowed you, but really we need to—'

'It's the truth,' she said, but deep down she knew that it was no good. She took the broken necklace from her pocket. 'There was a wolf. It tore this from Gwen. Nan made it for her.'

Nell stared down at the little necklace with its little moons, suns and stars. Every year a little iron necklace from Dru Church. She froze.

She sank back into the leather seat and stared straight ahead.

Iron.

Nan.

She reached for the door handle. 'Sorry. You're right. I'm making it up. I'll go.'

He reached over and slammed the door shut. The twin beams of his gaze found her again. He looked disgusted. 'This is not funny, Twigs.'

She hung her head as if in shame. 'I was attention-seeking, that's all. Pretending I knew something amazing. Ignore me.'

He turned the key and the dashboard lit up like the cockpit of an aircraft. 'I'll take you back to the

111

station. You can wait there.'

He put his arm on the back of the seat and reversed at speed down the alley. No, she hadn't time for him to take her there. She had to get out now.

'I'm going to be sick,' she cried.

He jammed on the brakes. 'Not in this car!'

'Then let me out.' She tried the door but he'd got central locking on. 'Right now. I'm having a panic attack. I can't breath.'

'I can't let you out. I have to take you somewhere safe.' He swore. 'You're a mess, Nell. Totally useless.'

Am I? she shouted back, but silently, the way she held most of her conversations with him. You don't know me, Dad, not at all.

'Take me to Nan's,' she pleaded. 'She can look after me.'

'Oh Lord, do I have to?' The steering wheel got one last thump. He didn't get on with his mother, they argued a lot. The Churches were dysfunctional. In the end he sighed and said, 'OK. To your nan's.'

She kept her head down. See, not so useless after all.

As Church did a super-fast sliding turn out on to the road, and then jammed his foot down on the gas and screeched forward, she glanced up and saw a group of girls walking towards her. It was Gwen's gang with Bria and Paige tagging along behind, filing down the road, sleepy-eyed like puppies, but perfectly colour co-ordinated, long hair blowing silkily in the cold breeze. They were coming to worship at the little altar they'd set up at the entrance to the wood. When they saw her in the car Bria and Paige's eyes narrowed, until they saw Church sitting beside her, and then they mouthed kind words and gave her tragic looks.

It's a wonder they didn't burst into flames for being so two-faced.

Eleven

The Red House wept gently in the damp morning air. Nell knew why it was made of iron now. It had been keeping the Watchers safe for years, and keeping her grandmother safe too.

'It's a bluff.'

'It isn't, Nan. It's for real. Evan told me.'

She'd always liked the house, with its rambling corridors and uneven floors. She liked sitting in the dusty library examining the crumbling old books, whilst a few folklore students searched the shelves, or sat hunched over old records.

Today she was in the kitchen. It looked the same and smelled of apples and wood smoke as it always did, but it didn't feel the same. There was tension in the air, and the murmur of voices drifting in from another room. Usually she would be sitting at the big pine table, eating biscuits, but not today. Now she was at one side of the kitchen and Druscilla Church was at the other, the letter clutched in her hands.

She'd thought that all she had to do was tell Nan, and then the camps would be opened immediately. But things were going wrong, very wrong.

'Nell, they lie to humans all the time. It's what they do. It's a point of honour to them.' Dru tried to smile but it didn't work. She wasn't the cuddly type of grandmother. She rode a motorbike. She took them to biker conventions and festivals, not to the park. She didn't read them girly stories, she read them bloody fairytales, the original ones, where the wolf ate Red Riding Hood and the only way to stop the girl in the red shoes dancing was to chop her feet off.

'You'll see,' she said. 'Fen will back down. He knows the consequences if he goes through with this.'

'Not this time,' said Nell desperately. 'I know Evan. He wouldn't lie to me. He was my friend.'

Dru scrunched the letter and threw it down. 'I don't think so. The Elven don't make friends with us, ever. They steal our girls, but make friends – no.'

'So all those stories you told us, about girls being taken by the fairy folk, the ones who disappeared and never came back . . .'

'Yes, all true. It was the Elf-King curse. Now it's been hijacked by Fen.'

Some of the shock had worn off, but Nell still felt as though she was living in a dream.

'I can't believe you're a Watcher,' she said bitterly. 'Me and Gwen called you Biker Nan, you were good, we never suspected. I thought you knew so many fairy stories because you were the head of the folklore society. Now I see where Dad gets his undercover policing skills from.'

Dru began to pace, her boots clattering on the red floor tiles. 'Last night I sensed something was going to happen,' she muttered. 'I should've done more. I should've gone and checked . . .'

'So put it right now,' said Nell, trailing after her. 'You have to! Open the camps and they'll give her back.' Dru said nothing. 'Did you hear me, Nan? Just give them what they want.'

Dru turned round. 'No. We cannot give in to their demands.' She took hold of Nell's shoulders. Her voice was calm and serious, but there was an undercurrent of grief. 'It breaks my heart, but we have to think of the greater good,' she said. 'We can't make an exception for Gwen.'

Nell felt her knees begin to shake. 'But she's your granddaughter!'

'I am the Head of the Watchers in this country. How would it look if I broke the rules?'

They both heard the front door open and footsteps walking down the hall. Voices spoke softly, then a face appeared in the doorway. It was a man Nell had seen before, usually sitting in the library.

'Any news?' he began. Behind him, two more faces peered in.

Dru waved him away. 'Go to the library. I'll be in soon.'

The man disappeared.

'He's a Watcher?' said Nell. 'And all those others I saw here?'

Dru carried on pacing. 'Yes. I've called an emergency meeting. Then we'll go to the mist. We'll negotiate.'

Nell felt like screaming. 'Talk – is that all? Don't you care about Gwen?'

Her grandmother's hands were twisting themselves together now, but her face was as hard as a marble statue. 'When you live with a secret like this one, you learn not to think of your own feelings.'

'Because you never had to lose a sister!' Nell howled.

Dru stopped and whirled round at her. 'You don't know what I lost,' she said sharply. 'Every Watcher has made hard choices.'

Nell choked back tears. 'What did you give up, huh?'

A spasm of pain crossed Dru's face. 'A life with my son, Tom. I was never there for him. I was always somewhere else, chasing Elven. Or meeting some prime minister or president to reassure them. And now look at the mess Tom's making of being a parent to you and Gwen!'

Nell thought her head was going to explode. This was ridiculous. 'Well, he won't have to worry about Gwen, if you DON'T OPEN THE CAMPS!' she screamed.

When her words had finished echoing round the kitchen, Dru pressed her hands to her face for a moment, then sighed and said, 'OK, you'd better come with me. I suppose you deserve to know the whole story – for a little while at least,' and marched her across the hallway.

Nell had never been inside Nan's study before. She and Gwen had tried to sneak in a few times, but the door was always locked, and the curtains drawn. Dru said she wrote her folklore books in there and didn't want her work disturbed.

Nell knew differently now. It was like the incident room during a police investigation.

There were rows of photographs pinned to the wall. She went over to them. Elven faces looked back at her, white-haired and dark-eyed, all of them her age or younger. They'd been caught on camera in the street, in the woods, coming out of shops, as though this was an identity parade of criminals.

'These are members of the Rivers great-family,' said Dru. 'Out of a hundred kin, only the younger ones are free now. And I'm responsible for what they get up to, because they use the mist in my wood.'

'There's more than one mist?'

'There used to be thousands. Now there are ten left in the world. Ten gateways spread throughout the cold countries of the North, each one leading into the Elven land. And ten great Elven families. Each great-family tends to stick to its own favourite country.'

Nell walked along the rows. The snaps had been taken with telephoto lenses, whilst the Elven were running away, or turning back to laugh triumphantly and jeer as they escaped into the woods. She ran her finger along them. There was the girl who'd followed her and Evan, her long plaits flying in an arc as she ran from the camera. Then a shot of a boy with long white hair who was holding a bow and arrow and aiming at the camera. Last in the row was the little boy who'd sat on the front of Evan's scooter, outside the school. He was being pulled along by two bigger girls with long white hair flying behind them, as they fled from the prying photographer. One image looked like a picture of a tree and nothing else, until she looked closely and saw a girl almost blended into the trunk, gazing into the camera like a startled deer.

'We can never catch them,' said Dru. 'The youngsters have this trick, flitting they call it. They move like the wind.'

Nell didn't answer. She was staring at a shot of Evan, a wild, fearless look on his face as he turned to shout at the camera. She touched her fingertip to it. 'We sat together at school.'

Dru put a sympathetic hand on her shoulder. 'He was checking you and Gwen out. Finding out your movements, and when they could snatch you.'

'We didn't have to talk. I didn't have to think up things to say. It was comfy. I thought I'd made a friend.'

Dru's hand squeezed. 'That's what they are – wild, charming and funny. Sometimes I think I'd rather spend an evening with the Elven than anyone else.' She smiled briefly. 'But if they become offended, or they take a dislike to you, then they'll show their claws. And if they think they've been betrayed, they'll seek vengeance for ever.'

She took Nell's chin and made her look away from the images and meet her eyes.

'The River brothers are dangerous, love. Dreadfully dangerous. They could take this world and break it into little pieces if they wished. They could take it from us completely.'

She turned Nell round and made her look at another set of photos. These were from CCTV and security cameras. Locations were scrawled on them – Brownhills Energy, North Yorks Generating Plant, EMEB substation. Nell guessed this meant they were taken from inside power stations.

'Between them they're trying to ruin this country. Ragnarok – the ultimate chaos. That's what Fen has threatened if they don't get their parents back.'

Dru's finger jabbed on to one blurry shot.

'That's him. That's Fen. Fenrir the wolf, they call him. He's the eldest, maybe twenty. He says he's a freedom fighter. But world leaders see him as a terrorist.'

It was a still from a security camera in black and white. A weird glow surrounded his body as though he pulsed with electricity. His head was turned towards the camera, and something seemed to be wrong with his eyes. One shone like an animal's, the other was a black hole. There was a hint of a mocking smile. He didn't look human, he looked eerie, like something you'd see on a paranormal website. It didn't help that he was half in, half out of a wall.

'Beware the Elven, for they are both substance and

shadow,' said Dru, in her witchy storytelling voice. 'And they walk through walls like ghosts of the night.'

Nell shivered. 'How?'

Dru shrugged. 'They're not human, that's all we can say. Fen can pass through any security barrier. And somehow he's taught himself to play games with the power grid – he can short out circuits or reroute the power. That's how he can write his name in light across our towns and cities.' She frowned at the picture. 'The Elven can always think up new ways to cause mischief to humans. But this time I think toying with electricity has fried Fen's brain.'

There were more photos of him, but these had been taken in nightclubs. In each one he had the same glowing outline, with a few zigzags inside, and the one shining eye.

'He says he hates all humans, but that doesn't stop him going after human girls,' Dru carried on, in a disgusted voice. 'He picks them up in clubs. The girls fall for him. Next morning he ditches them. They don't even remember meeting him.'

She pointed at another image, an outside shot taken from a CCTV camera. This one was of Evan climbing easily down the side of an enormous pylon.

'And now he's passing on his new skills with electricity

to his younger brother. Evan seems to be doing most of the sabotage these days.'

Nell thought back to how Evan looked after Rikstall's attack, as he was kneeling in pain, nursing his burned hand. He'd looked so helpless that she'd wanted to put her arm round him and comfort him. He hadn't looked like a terrorist or a freedom fighter.

Dru stared at the photos. 'Five years ago they started coming to our world and staying. They said that this was their home now! We don't know why. They won't talk to us. But we can't allow it.'

'So send them back to their land, then,' said Nell, desperately. 'Let them out of the iron camps.'

Dru shook her head slowly.

'We've always been able to send them through the mist, but we can't stop them coming back. That's why the Watchers were first formed. For centuries all we could do was keep an eye on them, and chase them back when they tried to rob us or make fools of us.' She smiled sadly. 'I remember when I became a Watcher, I used to see them at concerts or festivals, or dining in our restaurants. But living here permanently is different. It cannot happen. Imagine how scared people would be. Imagine the war that would break out!'

Nell wanted to argue and say there was room for

everyone – but she was thinking, oh lord, the Vicar looks at us as if *we're* from another planet when we sit on the church wall at nights. And half the old people in Rowan block are scared of the Jamaicans who've moved in. So what chance have the Elven got of being trusted?

Dru took Nell's hands and held them tight. 'So until we can find a way to send them back, and then block up the gateways permanently and end the problem for good, we have to keep them contained.'

Nell pulled away. 'But iron prison camps, Nan!'

Dru frowned. 'You think we're bad, you don't know what the world leaders wanted! There were orders to round up all Elven found in our world and get rid of them. For good. Genocide, Nell. Do you know what that means?'

'They wanted to kill them all.'

'Yes. Wipe out an entire species. When we found this out, we had to think fast. The iron camps are the only way to keep them safe for now.' She waved a hand at her passport and a folder of tickets on the desk. 'I've just come back from one of the camps. They're not ideal. But they will have to do, until we can lock the gateways in the mist for good.'

'I get it now,' said Nell. 'But none of this is Gwen's fault. And she's the one who's getting punished.'

'I know.' For a moment Dru's face sagged, and she looked older and broken. Then she took a deep breath and straightened her shoulders again. 'You have to understand, Watchers are like the police. We take an oath that we'll not give in to hostage-taking, bribes or threats. If we changed the rules, they would take hostages again and again. No one would be safe.'

'So Gwen disappears to save everyone else!' said Nell bitterly. 'I don't care about everyone else. I only care about her.'

Dru just stared at her. 'I'm sorry.' A phone rang from somewhere and was answered. Then a voice called for Dru. 'Hang on, I'll be back.'

Nell sat herself on the desk and stared bleakly at nothing.

So that's it, she thought. There's only me.

Somehow she had to find a way to get Gwen back.

The big hand of the clock on the wall jerked forward, with a loud tick. Eleven fifteen. Time was flying past. But an idea was beginning to form in her mind, twirling like a silkworm on a thread. It was stupid really, barely possible, but it was the only one she had.

First she had to get out of here.

When Nan came back in, she said, as casually as she could, 'Evan said we have until sundown. What

126

time's that, please?'

Dru sighed but went over to one of the desks, as Nell knew she would, and took out the old silver moonrise watch that she and Gwen had loved so much as a child. Instead of telling the time like a normal watch, it had a little moving sun and moon. As the sun revolved from left to right and eventually disappeared behind a night cloud, a moon would appear on the other side and begin its own revolution through a starry sky. It had been telling moonrise and sunrise for a hundred years, Nan claimed, and was very valuable.

'The sun sets at five o'clock this afternoon,' she said, peering at it.

Nell took the silver watch from her and stared at the slowly moving little sun. With every tick of the mechanism the sun jolted forward a tiny amount, closer to the cloud that would cover it. Just over five hours – that's all the time she had.

She slipped the watch into her pocket. Luckily Dru didn't notice because she was fiddling in the drawer for something else. Nell heard her murmur, 'I always wondered if you or Gwen would inherit the immunity to the Elven charm.'

'Now you know,' she said. 'I did. Gwen didn't.'

Dru turned round with a small black case in her hands.

Nell took a step back. She didn't like the look on her grandmother's face. It reminded of her of when Dru used to insist they took a spoonful of blackstrap molasses every time they visited – to make them healthy, apparently.

'Yes. You were unlucky,' Dru murmured. 'No one likes to think of their children or grandchildren having to know the things we know.'

'What's that?' said Nell, pointing at the case doubtfully.

Dru didn't answer. She put the case on the desk and opened it up. 'You're too precious to me. I can't lose both of you.'

It looked like the sort of kit used to pierce her and Gwen's ears. There was the same small, blue piercing gun, but instead of a row of studs or sleepers, there were some little metal staples in a twisty shape, like the maths symbol for infinity.

'What's going on?' she said.

Dru tried to smile. 'Something to make you feel better. It doesn't hurt. It's just a pinch.'

She was loading one of the infinity staples into the little blue gun now.

'What sort of something?' said Nell, her heart pounding.

'It's a treatment for those who have been exposed to the

Elven.' She came over and pushed a long strand of hair from Nell's face as she gazed down at her. 'It puts a little permanent implant under the skin of your right ear. It stops you being able to remember them.'

'So I would never remember meeting Evan?'

'It will seem like a dream, and then it will fade.' Dru smoothed the hair away from Nell's right ear. 'Poor Nell. Always the nervous one and yet you inherited the immunity. I wish it hadn't been you.' She took a firm grip on Nell's shoulder.

'Let go, Nan! I've got to go. Dad said I had to meet him—'

'No, he didn't' said Dru, increasing her grip. 'You have to stay here. You have to leave this to me and the other Watchers now. We'll go and we'll meet with Evan. We'll make Fen give Gwen up. I'm confident we will.'

But Nell could see that Dru's hand was shaking ever so slightly. She wasn't as confident as she was making out.

It was time to use some of Gwen's tricks. She could never cry prettily like Gwen, who sniffed daintily and her eyes went like diamonds and everyone wanted to hug her. No, when she cried tears slid down her cheeks and her face became blotchy. Then her nose would run. But there was no time to worry about things like that. She burst into messy, noisy, hideous tears.

'Nell, please stop it,' said Dru, hanging on to her arm. 'Crying won't get Gwen back, love.'

But Nell wasn't finished. If tears didn't bother Dru then she knew what would. She made herself retch.

'Oh help! I think I'm going to be sick,' she choked.

That made Dru let go. She wasn't the wiping-up-sick type of grandmother. 'Go to the bathroom, then. Splash water on your face. Then come straight back to me.'

Nell tottered out with her hand on her mouth, thinking, I'm getting good at this.

Upstairs, she leaned her hands on the washbasin and stared at herself in the big mirror. Her face was pale and smudged with mud. Her hair was a long tangled mess decorated with twigs and leaves. Her fur coat was filthy and the cuffs were wet.

Nan's right. I'm Nell the worrier, she thought. And I desperately want to do what I usually do when Gwen's screaming and making a fuss about something, or Mum and Dad are having one of their fights in the garden. I want to get out of this world and into my daydreams, become Hélène, skip away from it all, into a life that's problem free.

She pulled a sorry face in the mirror, then squared her shoulders.

Well, tough. I don't get to stay on the edges this time. There's no one else to save Gwen. This is down to me.

She felt in the pocket and pulled out the little broken necklace. It smelled of her sister's perfume – her silly, bossy sister, whose only ambition was to marry a footballer. Then she pulled out the moonrise watch. She stared at it, trying to get the plan straight in her mind.

It's not a very good one, she thought, but it's all I have.

It would mean she would have to do something that scared the life out of her. She would have to go into the Elven forest, amongst the brambles that tore at her hair and clothes, and the branches that seemed to reach for her with twiggy hands. And the wolves.

Could she do this, risk losing her world, her mum, her house, her life, and be banished to a place that shouldn't exist for ever? Could she become something else, something beyond wishing she was Hélène?

Yes. But first she had to get out of here.

She took off the fur coat and left it lying on the floor. Outside, hanging over the banister, was the leather biker jacket Nan kept here for her, so they could go riding on the Harley. Gwen wouldn't go near the motorbike, saying it was filthy and messed her hair and clothes up, but Nell loved clinging on to the back and feeling the wind rushing past and the ground going by so close beneath her feet. She put the jacket on and stowed the necklace in one pocket and the moonrise watch in the other. She looked in the mirror. She looked even thinner, but it had changed her silhouette, which was the aim. She'd read somewhere that small prey creatures have the outline of a hawk imprinted on their minds, so if they see a shadow in that shape, they scarper. Dru and the other Watchers had an imprint of her in a long fur coat on their minds. Maybe they wouldn't notice someone who looked like a young biker boy.

This gave her another idea. Next to the sink was a pot with a brush, comb and scissors in it. She took a deep breath and got to work.

After a few minutes' work, she crept downstairs. The hall was empty. She could hear Dru's voice coming from the library. Nan obviously thought she was too pathetic to do anything as impulsive as running away.

She quietly opened the front door and stopped.

The gravel driveway leading to the Red House was filling up with cars, and another one was pulling to a halt. The driver wound his window down and shouted to another couple who'd already parked their car and were heading towards the house.

'I got the alert. It's bad, isn't it?' one shouted.

'About as bad as it gets. Fen's done it this time.'

As they came towards the front door, she quickly slid behind a coatstand crammed full of old coats. The Watchers pushed the door open and walked straight past her, shouting for Dru.

As soon as the last one disappeared, Nell sprinted out of the front door and made for the road. Out of sight of the house, she hesitated.

The Red House was on one side of the sprawling Woodbridge Woods. Her house and the mist were on the other. If she cut through the wood it was quicker, a mile at the most, but she might lose her way. She couldn't risk it. She would have to take the road that ran round the outside, even though it was three times as far.

She set off. She'd done cross country at school, her skinny build was just right for it, but this was a longer run and she wasn't pacing herself. Every time a vehicle went by she had to scoot behind bushes or parked cars, using up valuable time. The road seemed endless, and after the first mile her breath ran out. So did her optimism. The full horror of what she was planning began to prey on her mind. It was impossible, it was stupid! She ran on, waiting for her second wind to kick in and the stitch in her side to go, but it didn't. It got worse.

She couldn't slow down. She had to find Evan before

they discovered her gone and followed.

Eventually, holding her side and grimacing, she swerved into Woodbridge Road, passing the corner shop that the secondary students used, and the low wall they sat on to eat their sweets. Tears pricked her eyes. Every lunchtime Gwen would sit on that wall with her friends, talking, laughing and blowing bubble-gum bubbles. She slowed down and went inside and bought a bottle of water and a few packets of green apple gum. She gulped half the water down and splashed the rest on her face. Then, as she carried on running, she took a piece of gum out and began chewing it. The smell shot up her nose and into her brain. It was the scent of Gwen. That's what she needed – a picture of Gwen in her mind, reminding her that she *had* to do this, stitch or no stitch, hope or no hope.

Still chewing, she ran by the school. It was closed for the weekend, but there was a BBC broadcast van outside, and a woman with a mic talking to the Head. Then the church came into view and she began to slow down to a jog and then to a walk, so that she didn't attract too much attention. She hardly dare look at the clock on its steeple.

Five minutes to twelve. She could make it.

At the entrance to the alley that led to the woods a policeman was walking up and down blowing on his hands and flapping his arms. Loops of crime-scene tape rattled. The sky hung low overhead, and a wickedly cold wind was whisking crisp packets about and making a discarded Coke can rattle across the ground. Up above, a helicopter hovered low over the trees, the beat of its engines blowing loud and then soft with the wind.

A few metres away the church car park was full of police cars and vans. All were locked, except the white forensics van parked at the back with its boot open. The team had packed up, ready to go back to their labs. They must have completed their fingertip search of the wood. They wouldn't have found anything, Nell knew. Why analyze a hair or a fingerprint – the Elven wouldn't be on a database. Their kit was stacked in boxes waiting to be loaded, but it gave her an idea. It was something that might make her crazy idea a little less dangerous.

First, though, she was going to have to make her way past Gwen's gang.

Twelve

'Oh my God,' said Paige. 'What have you done to your hair?'

They were all there, Becca, Fliss and the rest of them, with Paige and Bria hanging on as usual.

They'd been sitting on the churchyard wall, by a little shrine they'd made and decorated with candles and flowers. But they jumped down and surrounded her as she tried to walk by. They were all wearing the Saturday clothes according to the gospel of Gwen and had their hair in the proper Saturday ponytails. To be friends with Gwen you had to obey rules that she made up and added to all the time.

Certain colours had to be worn on certain days. No excuses or you got frozen out all day.

No trousers, except on Saturdays. If you broke the rule you sat on your own at lunch.

No one could wear a ponytail in the week. Bunches, plaits and headbands were all OK.

If you didn't obey the rules you got excluded for good, and even with Gwen missing they still obeyed. Now they were all around Nell, like sharks scenting blood, giving her sharp little glances and blocking her path.

'You cut your hair off!' said Bria, flicking a lock that now only reached to Nell's jaw. 'Doesn't suit you. Shows too much of your face.'

Nell kept quiet, looking from one face to the next. Not one was friendly.

'Is it for Gwen? To show you care?' said Becca. 'She always laughed at your hair.'

'It's so ragged,' said Paige disdainfully. 'Did you cut it with blunt scissors.'

'No, I went to Candy Heads,' said Nell, naming an expensive place in town. 'Their top stylist did it. It cost a fortune.'

Paige took another look. 'Yeah, well it's a good cut but your face ruins it.'

For a moment Nell felt embarassed for them all. They were so shallow. Why had she ever worried about them falling out with her?

'So? I don't care what you think.'

They looked shocked at this awful admission. Nell

wanted to hit them for being so stupid, but then Paige went for the kill.

'Is it true – you saw someone but you left Gwen on her own?' she demanded, her eyes alight with the horror of it all.

'Yes, but—'

'Why?' cried Paige. 'I wouldn't have left my worst enemy.'

'It was for a few seconds . . .'

Now Becca's baby-blue eyes became screwed up and small. 'What's up with you, Nell? Do you hate her or something?'

'No.'

She tried to get by but their circle tightened. Nell looked from one ice-pack stare to another.

'Jealousy makes people do bad things,' said Paige.

'Who says I'm jealous of Gwen?'

Paige twiddled a length of hair round and round her finger and gave Nell a sly look. 'Everyone.'

'No, they don't.'

Paige raised a perfect, Gwen-like eyebrow. She'd definitely been studying her heroine. 'You believe that. Cling to that thought.'

'We've done a Facebook page,' said Bria. 'What have you done?'

Becca stood in the way. 'Yeah, and what's with the clothes? Do you think you're Ninja girl or something?'

'Yes.'

Silence reigned for a moment. Lips began to smirk. Those sly glances went round the circle like some secret code, but she didn't care any more. So what if they talked behind her back – she wasn't going to be there to hear it. Their stupid, spiteful voices faded for the first time in months . . .

'Can I go?' she said. 'Or do you want something worse than a dead leg?'

'Bitch,' said Becca and reached out to grab her hair. That's how Becca always fought, hair-pulling and nails.

Nell jumped back. Her foot came up, and the Heavenly Strike struck. Not hard, but enough to sweep Becca off her feet and leave her sitting on the ground.

'Sorry, can't stop,' she said, stepping over her. 'I'm busy.'

Pulling the sleeves of her jacket over her hands to keep warm, Nell threaded her way through the police vehicles to the forensics van. Checking no one was around, she reached into a box and took one of the blue tracker torches that had been used to search for Gwen's blood. She stowed it in her pocket.

As she straightened up, she caught her reflection in the van window. The day was dull and grey enough for it to act like a black mirror. It showed her face with the stone wall of the church behind her. Only her darker features stood out – her eyes, her mouth now held in a tense straight line and the rag-doll, cropped hair. As she stared at herself the church clock high above began to ring out for midday.

Something flickered in the glass behind her and suddenly Evan was there.

'Stealing now, as well as breaking into other worlds?'

She turned round. He'd walked through the church wall as if it was a curtain. He put his head on one side and looked at her.

'You cut your hair. At last I can see you clearly.'

He was trying to be casual but his hands were twisting a couple of silver signet rings round and round on his thin fingers. He was wearing slouchy clothes, in the same colours as the autumn trees close by. He could've blended in and become invisible in seconds, except for that startling bright hair.

'Did Church send you with good news?' he said.

'She says you're trying to destroy our world.'

'Sabotage. Until we get the camps open.'

'But the power cuts scare people. They cause accidents.'

His face did one of its quick changes. He stuffed his hands in his pockets and peered at her through hurt eyes.

'How would you like someone to come and take your parents away, to not even know where they are being held, to not be able to ask one single person for help? You'd become a freedom fighter then, wouldn't you?'

She felt her own anger rise. 'Fen's making things worse not better. And he's dragging you into it. The Watchers have got photos of you.'

Evan held his arms out helplessly. 'It can't get any worse for us. He's going for Ragnarok, Nell. He's trained me, and now I have to help him bring chaos. I go round and throw switches at substations and rip out cables. Anything to disrupt the human world.' He kicked the van wheel irritably. 'I hate it. Please say this is all over and Church is going to open the camps in exchange for Gwen, so I can forget about electricity.'

She looked him squarely in the eye and forced herself to smile. If her plan was to work, he had to believe her next words.

'She's really angry, but of course she agreed. Gwen's her granddaughter.' It gave her a pain in the heart to say it like that, when it was so far from the truth.

Nothing happened for a couple of heartbeats, then

142

Evan let out a long relieved breath that blew his hair upwards. 'I knew she would. I told the others.' He put a hand to his heart. 'I swear we all thought Fen had gone too far. But he said the Watchers would have to back down.' He looked around. 'Is she meeting us here?'

This was it. Nell hoped her voice wouldn't wobble. 'No. She has lots of arrangements to make. But she insists that I go with you to get Gwen. Then she'll meet us at the mist before darkness falls. You'll get the addresses of the camps and you'll be able to speak to the freed Elven by mobile.'

For the first time in ages his crooked grin appeared. 'You needn't go all the way to the palace,' he said. 'I can fetch her. It'll be quicker that way.'

'No, she insists I have to go. To keep Gwen safe and stop her panicking.'

His grin faded and he looked puzzled. 'She wants you to go into our forest? She'd risk that?'

'It's for Gwen,' said Nell, crossing her fingers behind her back. 'She loves her and she'd do anything to keep her safe.'

He shrugged, as if he'd believe anything of humans. 'OK, then. If that's what you want.'

Nell didn't know whether to be relieved or angry that he'd swallowed the lie. Maybe even he thought

Gwen was more worthy.

But then he gave her a long look and said, 'It's pretty brave of you, Nell. You've seen our world. It's dangerous for humans. Get lost in it and you'll be stuck there for ever.'

'I'm not brave. I'm petrified.' It was true. She couldn't stop shaking and it wasn't the cold.

'Would Gwen do the same for you?' he said curiously.

'No!' It was her turn to laugh. 'She'd hold a candlelit vigil, though. Her and her friends, looking lovely in colour co-ordinated outfits.'

He started off towards the alley. 'Come on then, if you dare.'

But to Nell's horror she could hear a motorbike speeding down Woodbridge Road, and it was getting louder by the second. It was Druscilla's, she'd recognize it anywhere. Nan was on her trail.

'Wait!' she called urgently. 'Church said you can move really fast.'

He came back. 'She's right. We can move faster than the wind. We can outrun the dawn if we have to.'

'Can you take me too?'

'Easy.'

The pitch of the bike engine changed as it slowed near the church. Maybe Dru was asking Gwen's gang if they'd seen her. They'd only have to point this way.

She moved closer to him. 'Do it.'

He put his arms round her. 'Hold tight,' he whispered.

And then she had no breath to say any more. The air hit her like concrete.

Thirteen

Speed. Impossible speed. She was moving so fast that the force trapped her arms to her side and stopped her moving, like a straitjacket. She couldn't twitch even a finger.

Then her back hit something hard and every atom of air left her body with an *ooph*. The world stopped. Nothing, nothing, nothing and then she fell to her knees and – at last – sucked in another breath. Relief was short-lived, though, as her stomach lurched. She was going to be sick – for real this time.

It was hideous. Gwen said that there was never any need to throw up in front of anyone. If any of her gang dared to, then they'd be cold-shouldered straight away. Well, there was nothing Nell could do about it. She fell to her knees and was sick. She prayed for a miracle, that Evan had moved away and not noticed. But no such luck.

His hand reached down and held a lock of her newly shorn hair out of the way.

'Sorry,' he said, ruefully. 'It can get humans like that on the first go.'

'It's me that's sorry,' she gasped. 'Rollercoasters do the same. And car trips. And the sea.'

She waited, crouched, for what seemed like an hour before she could breathe properly again. Then she staggered to her feet.

'That wasn't running, that was supersonic flying.'

He grinned. 'It's flitting. It's why we can't be caught.'

She looked at him. He was skinny and twitchily athletic. She'd seen him leaping fences at school and doing back-flips with ease. But he didn't look like someone who could run like the wind whilst carrying a girl. 'So how does it work? Is it supernatural?'

'I'm not telling a human! The Watchers think they know everything about our powers. But they don't.' He gave her a wicked smile. 'We've got lots of surprises.'

'No wonder you freak people out,' she said. 'If you can move that fast, and walk through walls, and make people forget you.'

He shrugged. 'True. But we're like our brother and sister wolves. We could strike down humans easily – but we don't.'

'Good!'

She looked around. The wild run had somehow got them past the police and the media, and straight through the mist. She was standing in the same clearing as last night, with the forbidding forest in front of her. The music was still playing. Lilting harmonies and melodies were blowing about in the air. Shreds of mist were stuck to her clothes and face like damp tissue paper. The dull clouds had gone away. She was under a bright blue Elven sky, and although the sun was shining down it only made the paths between the trees look even darker.

Somewhere within that darkness was Gwen.

'Where to?' she said hurriedly. 'Which path?'

'Wait. Chill. I'll get our guide,' he said. He began whistling and calling for Faolan, who was a grey shadow, sniffing around on the other side of the clearing.

Whilst his attention was on the wolf, she slipped the silver moon watch from her pocket. The little sun had passed the halfway point of the dial and was sliding its way downwards towards its cloud. Four hours to sundown, then Gwen would be lost to them for ever. This forest would be her only home.

And not just Gwen – me too, she thought with a shiver. But she'd done it now, she'd lied to Evan, she was in the mist again. She could only go forward.

'What's that?' he said.

She jumped, caught off guard. He was watching her again. He reached over and tried to take the watch.

She pushed his hand away and put it back in her pocket. 'Nothing.'

A growl vibrated close to her legs. She looked down into a pair of hostile, amber eyes. She hadn't even seen her move, but Faolan was now crouched next to Evan. Nell recognized the growl and the stare. They said *he's mine, keep away*.

Evan had his hand on the thick mane of fur round her neck, as though she was just a normal dog. It suited him, Nell thought, to be in the forest with a wolf at his feet.

'Pretty wild sister you've got there,' she said.

'We've always lived alongside wolves, ever since this land was made for us. We can even speak to them.' He stroked Faolan's rounded ears and made soft wolf noises. She leaned her head against him and gave a puppyish grunt of delight in reply. 'We're wolf whisperers. When we realized humans would always try to destroy us, we chose to make some wolves our kin. They've never let us down.'

'If you say so,' said Nell doubtfully.

She'd never been a dog person. She liked cats better, they didn't demand attention, they sat and watched like she did. Maybe she was radiating nervousness, because Faolan was watching her as if she was prey.

'You should make friends with her before we set off,' Evan said, with a challenge in his voice. Even he could see that she wasn't keen. 'I always cross the forest with her, she lets me know of any dangers.'

What can be more dangerous than a wolf? thought Nell, but she kept the thought to herself. If it took befriending Faolan to get her sister back, then she'd have a go.

'Hey,' she said awkwardly.

Faolan began to growl again, deep in her throat. One side of her mouth curled silently, showing a sharp white fang.

Evan was watching, so she tried again. She reached a hand forward. Faolan's teeth clicked together, so close she felt the heat of the wolf's breath.

Mine!

Nell held up her hands in surrender but she didn't move back. She forced herself to crouch down so their eyes were on the level. Unfortunately that meant Faolan's fangs were level too, but she brushed the thought aside and looked deep into those amber eyes.

Me and you need to get something straight, she told the wolf silently. I'm not competing. Soon he will be all yours again.

The wolf continued to stare without blinking, then turned away and hopped towards the trees.

Nell wasn't sure whether she'd scored a point or not. She stood up.

'Hmm,' said Evan. 'Not sure if that worked.'

Nell shrugged. 'I tried. Why does she limp – is she hurt?'

'No. She was born lame. She couldn't keep up with the other pups, so she became the omega, the lowest wolf, the one who gets pushed out of the pack. I rescued her.'

'That was a kind thing to do.'

'She was on her own and being a lone wolf is not good. Wolves are like us. They need their pack around them. We all need family.'

Pity you took Gwen from hers, then, she thought.

Evan gave Faolan another pat. 'I like things that aren't perfect.'

No wonder he gets on with you, then, Hélène whispered spitefully in her ear. Now stop hanging around, worrying about the forest, and go rescue Gwen.

She looked at the mass of trees and the dark paths leading into their heart.

'Is the big white wolf here, too?' she said.

'Thor? No. He's loyal to Fen.'

That was one blessing, then. She really didn't want to meet that blue-eyed monster amongst those trees.

She stuck her hands in her pocket and felt the smooth shape of the moon watch. She could almost feel the little sun ticking slowly downwards.

'We have to get going,' she said. 'Can you flit again? We'd be there in no time.'

'No. Too much of a strain, with you in my arms.' He grinned. 'First time I've ever hugged a human.'

'Big deal,' she said, trying to be cool like Gwen. But truthfully she could still feel the press of his arms around her.

He squinted up at the sky. 'We've got time to walk through the forest. Don't worry. We'll get Gwen back before sunset.'

He pointed to a narrow path, more like a dark tunnel through the undergrowth.

'We go this way.'

All around her the trees rustled ominously. She could hear things moving amongst the trees, out of sight. She really wasn't looking forward to going in there. 'I can't believe you dare live amongst all these wild creatures.'

'This is our land, Nell,' he called, as he made for the path. 'It's full of dangers and things that could attack. This is what your world was like a thousand years ago.'

As she followed him, she looked back, making sure that she would recognize the clearing again and be able to find the mist quickly. She'd need a quick exit when she got back. If she got back. The mist didn't show up so well in the daylight. Then she saw the white, writhing cloud peeking out from between two pine trees with lanterns swinging from their branches. She'd remember that. But then her eye caught another patch of mist a few metres farther along. She frowned and spun round on her heel. There was another, farther back, and some more over to her right.

Which one had she come through? She counted – not one mist but ten!

Of course. Ten gateways, ten families. But Nan had told her they were in different countries.

'Evan!' she called. 'Wait.'

She heard him crunching back over the carpet of pine needles. 'I thought you were in a hurry?'

She was, but she had to know which mist led to her wood. She couldn't tell him that though. 'I'm obsessive, I have to know things,' she said. 'I know that the mists are gateways, but they're side by side. How come, when Nan told me that they lead to different countries?'

'She's right.' He started pointing. 'That one leads to Siberia. That one to Canada. That one to Sweden . . .'

'No, not possible. Stop messing around,' she interrupted. She couldn't take his jokes at a time like this. 'Canada and Siberia and Sweden are thousands of miles apart.'

He started to look wicked again. 'You don't get it, do you, Nell? You don't realize how far away from home you really are. We're outside your world. We're outside your time. We're floating free. From here, all your countries are a patch of mist away. Think of them as magic doors. Make a wish and hey presto! – you're somewhere else.'

She pointed to one patch of mist. 'I walk through that and I'm in Canada?'

'That one? No. That's Alaska.' He grinned. 'Cheap travel to anywhere in the world, Nell. As long as it's cold and forested!'

'Which one leads to my wood?'

He pointed. She consigned it to her memory. The tree nearest to it had a trunk blasted by lightning. That was her exit.

'Come on, if you're coming,' he said, and he disappeared into the forest again.

She had to run to catch him up. As the forest closed round her, noises came at her from every angle.

'Watch yourself,' he called. 'It's pretty thorny at the start.'

He wasn't kidding. She was surrounded by brambles. Not just any old brambles, but the most lethal ones she'd ever seen. They had thorns three inches long and hooked at the tip. Good, they would be useful to her. She let her hand scrape over one of the thorns.

She couldn't stop herself saying, 'Ow!'

Suddenly he was there at her side again, as if he cared. She tried not to let him see that her finger was dripping blood. The little crimson drops were falling to the forest floor and becoming lost in the tangle of pine needles and grass.

'Carry on like this and you'll be cut to shreds before we get there,' he said.

'It's only blood.' She let the drops fall, exactly as she'd planned.

He sighed at her town-girl ways, and set off at a fast pace, maybe to teach her a lesson. The path was narrow so he walked in front, moving easily whilst she stumbled and tripped. The air was tinted green by the thick canopy of branches overhead. It was as though they were moving underwater.

The deeper they went, the worse it got. On either side there were sharp twigs and more thorns. She pulled the sleeves of her jacket over her hands and pushed her way through. Roots and creepers caught at her ankles. Insects buzzed in her face. She couldn't go two steps without jumping or looking round. When something hit the back of her legs, she almost screamed as she stumbled out of the way, but it was only Faolan sailing by, her ears back, her nose in the air. An unfriendly wolf, a hostile forest – this was going to be tough. Around her the trees rustled, creaked and murmured, above the endless rippling notes of the music. Every so often spears of sunlight lanced down through the branches high above and pierced the darkness. And the further she went, the more she began to feel that someone was watching her. Maybe someone was – all those exits, one for each great-family.

She stumbled into a run and caught up with him.

'You know the other great-families – are they here in the forest?' she said uncertainly.

She didn't fancy running into an adult Elven who might hate humans. She was having enough trouble with the wildlife, and getting ripped to shreds by brambles.

'You've been talking to the Watchers,' he said over his shoulder.

'Tell me about them,' she said, brushing something with lots of legs off her boot. 'It'll take my mind off the big insect that's trying to crawl up my leg.'

She heard him laugh. 'OK, town girl. Besides the Rivers,

there's the Dells, Willows, Moons, Snows, Heaths, Leafs and Meadows.'

She scrambled over a fallen trunk covered in toadstools that he'd leaped with ease. 'That's only eight.'

'The other two – the Stones and the Thorns – have gone to the Ice.' He said it like it was something terrible.

'And that means what – they've turned to ice? They live at the North Pole?'

He waved a hand around. 'This forest is huge, it goes far, far beyond where the sun shines, to the lake where it's always winter. That's where the Ice Elven live.' She saw him shiver. 'You don't want to know about them, believe me. Our mamas used to scare us with them, to make us behave.'

Stones and Thorns. Even their names sounded hard and dangerous.

'And the other seven?'

'We lost touch with them when the Watchers started imprisoning us. We don't know whether they've been captured or whether they're free in your world but can't get back in here. They're definitely not in the forest or they'd be helping us.'

He skipped over another fallen tree trunk and disappeared up the dark path beyond.

She felt in her pocket for the moon watch and glanced

at it. The sun was still ticking its way towards its cloud. How long had they been travelling? And how much further had they got to go? She had no way of knowing; all she could do was keep calm and keep stumbling forward.

She hurried after him. She still felt she was being watched, despite what he'd said. Why should he tell her the truth? She was lying to him, after all.

She stepped over a dead rabbit lying on the path.

And another thing that was distracting her – apart from the time ticking away and the insects crawling up her sleeves – was the music. There were no other sounds coming from the forest now, just that endless, maddening melody. It was really loud, beating at her eardrums. She sidestepped a dead crow. In fact she had the feeling the music was making her eyes vibrate. Either that or everything around her had started shaking.

She stopped. The trees were getting bigger too. The path in front of her, dappled with a rare splash of sunlight, had divided in two to go round an enormous tree trunk. It was so wide and old it looked as though it was made of stone not wood.

She clapped her hands to her ears. Where was the music coming from? She looked around. Everything was out of focus now, trembling to the melody. A creeper, leading from high up on the massive trunk to the ground, was pulsing so fast it was a blur. She stared at it, rubbing her eyes. It wasn't a creeper, it was a cable made of some kind of twisted metal. It was like the ones that hold telegraph poles up, but as thick as her arm. It was blurred because it was vibrating like a violin string.

'Is that making the music?' she murmured.

She put a hand out to touch it – but it didn't happen. Something hit into her. It was Evan. His arms were around her again. He pushed her back a few steps, and then let her go. They moved quickly apart.

'What did you do that for?' she shouted, above the music.

He pointed over to the cable. 'Don't touch it or you'll die.'

'What's a cable doing in a forest?'

'It's not a cable. It's the string of a harp.'

'Not the sort of harp I know,' she said. 'Not with a string that size.'

He pointed. 'See the massive tree trunk? It's not, it's a harp. It's just too big to see.'

She followed his pointing finger and looked up and up. The big trunk in the middle of the path disappeared through the canopy of pine branches high above them, and then carried on rising into the sky.

'It's so high its top has its own cloud,' he said, as they craned their necks.

She shaded her eyes. She could see more of the thick strings stretching down through the trees. 'Why would you have a giant musical harp here?'

'There's lots. They surround the forest, they keep it twisted out of your world.'

'These are your powerful devices? Poles with strings that hum a tune?'

'You never heard of magic harps?' He began leading her round the string.

'Yes, but in fairytales. The ones that make people dance or laugh or sleep for ever.'

'Sound has power,' he said. 'Sound can do amazing things. It can even kill.' He turned and walked off down a side path. 'That's why the strings are lethal. One touch and you're dead. I almost forgot you weren't Elven and didn't know.' He motioned her to follow him. 'I'll take you the long way round to be safe.'

'But we haven't time!' she said, starting to panic. They couldn't afford detours. 'It can't be that bad. How many strings are there?'

'A hundred. If you could sit on top of a tree, you'd see them coming down to the ground all around us. It would be as dangerous as walking through a minefield for you.'

'I don't care,' she said. 'I learn fast. Just lead me through them.'

'Keep close to me, then,' he said, and held out his hand. She took it and he led her through the tangle of singing cables that criss-crossed their path. It slowed them down, though.

Come on, come on, Nell willed. Please get me through this quickly. When they were nearly at the end and she could see that the way ahead was clear, the music suddenly paused. The silence was deafening.

'Oho,' said Evan.

'What?'

A second later the music started again, but the first few notes were harsh and off key. They grated, squealed and screeched like fingernails down a blackboard. They jarred her ears. She winced in pain. A few metres away a small bird fell to the ground in a flurry of feathers.

'It's not tuned right!' she said, as she ducked and followed him under another string.

She felt his hand tighten on hers. He probably didn't even realize he was doing it.

'That's because all the harps are failing, Nell.'

'They're stopping? Does it matter?'

He didn't answer for a moment. Then he said, in a flat voice, 'It means that our land will die.'

She stopped. 'Oh, lord.'

He turned back to her. 'What?'

'I know now. I see.' She stared at him. 'If this place dies, you'll have nowhere to live – unless you move back to our world.'

He stared into the forest. 'Yep,' he said, reluctantly. 'Pretty much.'

Nell squeezed his hand. 'Why didn't you tell the Watchers? They don't know!'

He shook her hand away. 'Oh, right. Why didn't we think of that?' he said, suddenly bitter. 'Because then the countries of the world would welcome us like old friends, huh? We tried to do it quietly but they noticed. If they knew this land was failing, they'd kill us rather than have us share the world, they're that scared of us!'

He put his hand on her head and ducked her under the last string.

'Can't you mend them?' she said, turning to look back at them.

'No. They were made by the Vanir.'

There was no time to ask, but she couldn't help herself. 'Who're they?'

'Elven who have lived over a thousand years,' he said shortly. 'Their skin goes like marble. Their eyes like black sapphires. Their power is incredible, they're almost gods.'

He carried on down the path. It was wider now, after the harp, so she caught up with him and walked by his side.

'So ask the Vanir to mend them.'

'They've gone. We don't know where,' he said, his voice still flat. 'Our parents tried to fix the Harps, but it didn't work. We don't know how any more.' He looked around. 'Sometime in the future there'll be no more Elven land. But not just yet, touch wood.'

To her surprise he reached out and tapped the trunk of a tree as they went by.

'You're superstitious?' she said. Anything to change the subject and make him look less miserable.

'No, I'm serious,' he said. 'We touch a tree to keep the spirit of the woods happy.'

'You really believe that?' she asked.

'No. I know it. Wood spirits can get very moody.' His grin was back. 'You have to appease them all the time.'

She looked at him doubtfully. 'You're joking. Aren't you?'

'No. Everything has a spirit, didn't you know? A flock of birds has a spirit. That's how they can migrate for thousands of miles to the same spot even when they've never done the trip before. A beehive has a spirit that looks after all the bees. And a wood has a spirit as well, that looks after all the trees.'

Nell looked around as she followed him. Maybe it was the wood that seemed to be watching her. If so, it didn't feel as though it liked her very much. They were deep inside the forest, and no spears of sunshine pierced the green shadows now. She fell over time after time. Sometimes he saved her, sometimes he didn't. When the path became wet she slipped and slithered, and got messier with every step. Evan didn't. The twigs didn't catch his clothes, the mud didn't stick to him. He moved like a cat, always knowing where his feet were, almost dancing over the snaking roots and creepers. Things crashed away from them; big, heavy things. Smaller things scuttled, weird insects buzzed in her face, loud screeches made her heart thump. Eyes blinked in the bushes and then disappeared. All around, the undergrowth rustled.

At one point he suddenly grabbed her arm and pulled her back. A moment later a big bone spun down from above and smashed to the ground inches from her.

'Lammergeyer,' he said.

Something huge and feathered took off from a branch above her head and crashed through the canopy of branches in an explosion of talons and funeral-black plumage.

'We call them bone breakers because they feed on

marrowbone and get it out by flying up high and dropping the bones on to rocks – or people's heads.'

'This is just how I imagined a fairytale forest. It's like a nightmare,' she said, as it smashed its way into the upper air and flapped heavily away.

'Don't worry, the Watchers'll wipe your mind when this is over,' he said.

She glanced sideways at him. 'You know about the treatment?'

'Yes. I bet you'll be glad. The Elven are a hard thing to know about. Keeping secrets separates you from other people.'

'Tell me something new,' she said. 'I was born feeling separate. I look at everyone else and they seem to understand the rules of our world – the way to talk, the right answers to give, when to take something seriously, when to laugh. I always get it wrong.'

'Not this time. You've persuaded your grandmother to agree to the deal.'

I wish, Nell thought, and would have worried about her plan and how it was going to work, but over to her left, there was a noise like something big was dying in agony. She could hear branches snapping, then something moaned, sending a flock of birds wheeling into air, wings humming. Faolan, who'd been walking at Evan's heel like a well-trained pet dog, shot off to investigate.

'Jeez, what's that?' she whispered, horrified.

'A stag bellowing, towngirl. This is the real forest. There are eagles, wolves, stags and bears. It's a forest from primeval times, never cut down, and never altered. It's not changed for a thousand years.' He looked around. 'Nothing much changes in the Elven world.'

He walked on and she began hurrying after him as the unseen stag crashed closer and bellowed again.

'I saw you with a mobile. And listening to an iPod.'

'We raid your world for gadgets. Fen's trying to find a way to make mobiles work in the forest. He's already got us power.'

Fen, Fen, Fen. Fen with his freaky glowing eye. She was already sick of hearing about Fen.

'Do I get to meet him?'

He'd gone a few steps before he answered. 'I suppose you'll have to. He can be a bit fidgety with humans. But when he knows that the Watchers have agreed, you'll see the best side of him.' His voice betrayed him, though. He sounded uncertain.

But Fen was in the future. She was more worried about who was trailing them now. It wasn't her imagination. Twice she'd seen a flash of white deep in the trees.

She walked closer to Evan. 'Is someone following us?'

He looked around casually. 'Nothing to be worried about. I'd know if we were in danger.' He thumped her arm gently. 'Anyway, you're as brave as any Elven boy.'

'I'm not a boy.'

'You're as good as.'

She shook her head. 'Wrong. I'm as good as a girl.'

He thought about that. 'True. You are as good as an *Elven* girl. You wait till you meet them. They're tough, like you.' He hesitated, then said, 'Remember the little Elvling on the scooter – Bean?'

'Yes.'

'He thought you were my girlfriend.'

Nell kept walking, her face straight and her gaze steady. Blushing seemed to have become a thing of the past with her. What was the use in the middle of a forest, her face wet with dew, her clothes stuck with pine needles and splattered with mud?

'He was so wrong,' she said lightly.

'Well, he's too young to know that Elven and human don't mix,' he said. She could tell he was trying to get a reaction out of her. 'He doesn't realize that the world would probably explode or something, if human and Elven ever got together.'

She nodded seriously. 'Good job we're not interested.'

He grinned. 'Absolutely. Wouldn't want the world

exploding.'

'Nope.' She looked at him innocently. He wasn't the only one who could be tricky. 'You'd better warn your brother, though. I heard he dates human girls.'

Evan looked away. 'Yeah, I heard,' he said quietly. 'But he's not himself. He's changed. He gets headaches that drive him insane. He hits his head against a tree trunk over and over again because they're so bad. I think it's the stress of all this fighting.'

One mention of Fen and he looked dejected, she noted.

They carried on, and after a while she heard the sound of fast running water, and she realized she was madly thirsty.

'I wish I'd brought a drink,' she said.

He pointed through the trees at a patch of bright sunlight.

'What's up with water?'

The sound of the rushing stream filled the little clearing as it cascaded over rocks into a crystal-clear pond. The grass was a bright emerald green from all the spray.

'Seriously,' she said, trailing after him. 'We don't have time to stop!'

'We do.'

'We don't!'

For the first time since they'd entered the forest, sunlight streamed down on them. It was a relief to be able to walk freely, without tripping over creepers and tree roots. Faolan ran ahead of them and began to lap the water noisily. As they followed her, something came out of the trees opposite. For a moment, Nell forgot the time. She forgot Gwen.

'You're kidding,' she breathed.

It was a pretty Arab pony, dapple grey, its hooves clattering over the rocks and pebbles. Just a pony, except that it had a long horn spiralling from its forehead.

'No, they're myths,' she murmured.

Evan eyed it warily. 'The Elven are myths and we're real.'

For the first time in what felt like days, Nell smiled.

'It's so beautiful!'

She crept closer, wishing she had a polo mint to offer it. Did unicorns like mints like normal ponies?

'So if this forest was once in our world – then we had unicorns too!'

'No, they only exist here,' said Evan, following her. 'The Vanir probably put them here as a joke. Then stories of them leaked out into your world. They didn't get the details right, though.'

It had stopped on the edge of the pool. Instead of drinking it was now watching them, in the twitchy, flighty way of all horses. The fabulous silvery horn sparkled in the sunlight.

'Watch out,' he said.

'Why? It's awesome.'

The unicorn fixed its gaze on her and lowered its head. Suddenly it didn't seem so pretty any more. A nerve twitched irritably on its white, dappled shoulder. Then it moodily scraped its dainty front hoof across the rock. Evan grabbed her arm.

'Awesome and bad-tempered,' he warned.

It leaped the pool, sending water spraying everywhere, and charged towards them. He pulled Nell back just in time. Even Faolan, who'd been noisily lapping water, shied out of its way. Before it could wheel round and stab them with its horn, Evan ran forward and smacked it hard on its rump. It took off, bucking and rearing, and disappeared into the trees again.

'Good riddance,' he said.

He knelt by the pool, and cupped a hand into the water and drank. Faolan came and curled herself at his feet. Nell stared after the unicorn.

'This is shattering a lot of my dreams,' she said. 'I'd always wanted unicorns to be real, and when they are, they turn out to be mean.'

'Life's not fair,' he said. 'Come and get a drink. We've got time. It's not far now.'

She sat down next to him, trying to relax. Trying not to think of the moon watch ticking away in her pocket. How far was *not far*?

He splashed his hand in the clear water. 'I thought you were thirsty.'

She hesitated. 'There's all kinds of bugs in water,' she said doubtfully.

'Not here. No industry. Just forest. Nothing to pollute it.'

The water was teeth-tinglingly cold. Nell leaned over and drank some, then sat back on her heels.

'You're right. It is good.'

Evan hugged his knees, the sun bouncing off his hair and skin, making him glow.

'You would have liked Elven life before they started arresting us.' He looked around as though he was a prince of the forest. 'Nothing troubled us. Nothing was serious. There were birthdays, holidays and weddings. All the great-families would meet for them. And the matchmaker would be there, helping the older ones choose who they were going to marry.'

'You have matchmakers?'

172

'Believe me. And the parties! All Elven know each other, so our parties are huge and wild. We used to travel through the mists, meeting up in woods and forests in different countries. Sometimes we'd come into the cities.' He smiled at her. 'I could have sat next to you at the cinema, or been in the next lane at the bowling alley, and you would never have guessed who we were. We never let ourselves be found out, and the Watchers kept their distance.'

She needed to hurry, but she couldn't stop herself wanting to hear about his life. 'Then it all changed?'

'When the harps began to fail, some Elven started moving into your world. At first no one noticed, then the Watchers began to round us up. Every time we left the mist we were in danger. Now if we dare travel through your world we have to flee in the dead of the night.' He gave a laugh but there was no humour in it. 'It's a good job Elven like starlight because we see a lot of it now.'

'What happened to your parents?'

He dabbled his hand in the water, and she thought he wasn't going to answer. Then he looked at her.

'They were betrayed by your grandmother and the Watchers.'

He started talking, slowly at first as though he'd never

spoken about it before.

'My little sister's name is Duck. She'd be five now. She was so cute, she had this whoosh of hair sticking straight up as though she'd touched something static.' He smiled as he remembered, but it didn't last long.

'It was her second birthday, and we were giving her a party, but first my father had to meet the Watchers. He arranged a truce. See, my father is the king.'

'Crikey,' said Nell. Hadn't she just thought that he looked like a prince? And he'd certainly acted that way at school – but she'd never thought it was true. 'You're royalty?'

He picked up a pebble and began to chip away at another rock. 'No, not exactly. Being an Elven king or queen is more of a risk than an honour. You end up as a go-between with humans on one side and Elven on the other. You're the scapegoat. That's why my father had to go and talk to the Watchers.'

He chipped away with the pebble. Strange shadows were moving on his face as he talked. At first Nell thought it was the sun dappling down through the high branches that overhung the stream.

'Dad was going to try to come to a compromise with the Watchers. See if they'd give us a piece of land for ourselves, and we'd keep to it. Church had arranged for him to meet her bosses in London. She'd promised that they would keep to the truce, so we all decided to go, as a treat for Duck. We sat at a pavement café, enjoying the sunshine, watching the world go by.'

More shadows settled on his face. 'But she'd tricked us. When the Watchers came it was to capture us and send us to an iron camp.'

'Why would Nan do that?' said Nell, horrified.

'To teach other Elven a lesson. To say – look out, we can catch the Rivers, so don't come to our world any more.'

He smashed the pebble down and it shattered. He didn't seem to notice. The shadows on his face grew deeper and changed colour – dull blue, purple, yellow, green, like colours found in an oil spill.

'All I could think was that it was Duck's birthday and the shouting was upsetting her. She was sitting on my knee, eating ice cream.' He looked at Nell. 'The next moment the street was filled with Watchers on motorbikes and in cars. They'd even got a helicopter buzzing overhead in case we managed to run for it.'

'They caught you all?'

He gave a laugh but it was more of a choke. 'They had us cornered, there in the middle of London. People at the other tables must have thought we were a bunch of criminals wanted by the police. They saw my father being pinned to the ground, and my mum fighting free only to be overcome by three or four of them and thrown into the back of the unmarked van they'd brought with them, cuffed in iron.'

'Why didn't you flit?'

'They'd moved iron barriers around us, before we noticed. Fen was like a madman, he was lashing out at them all. He was moving so fast they could hardly see him, but he couldn't get out. We could run but not far. I tried to run with Duck. But they came for me.' Something glinted on his eyelashes. A tear? 'They took her out of my arms, Nell! My little sister. I wasn't quick enough.' He bit his lip, drawing blood. 'Fen's right, I should've been quicker,' he muttered. 'I could hear her screaming in terror. She was scared to death. So I fought them.'

The shadows on his face thickened and she saw what they were – they were the ghosts of the bruises he'd suffered that day. His skin was remembering what the Watchers had done to him. When he looked at her now, one of his eyes was half closed and blackened.

'Fen saved me. He grabbed me and we ran, scattering the tables and the waiters. We went into the café, out of the back door, over the wall and through the yards. We got round the iron that way, and we got free.' He rubbed a hand over his face, wiping away the wetness. 'But I've never seen my parents or Duck since that day.'

He sat back, his face still a mess of purple and yellow bruises glowing on his white skin.

'Since then they've rounded up most of the adults. But they don't often get the young Elven. We're too fast. It's like trying to catch mice. Luckily our mamas teach us to stand up for ourselves, to live on our own. Thank Gaia, because it's the only way we've survived. But Fen swore that day that he would get revenge. That he'd close the camps and get everyone out. That if humans didn't let us share the world, then he'd take it from them.'

Nell said nothing. She didn't know what to say to a story like that.

'I saw a picture of one camp,' he continued. 'The iron fences are so high, and they're in the middle of a frozen wasteland, thousands of miles from anywhere, with one road leading to it. There are no trees. And the stars are blocked out by the lights that burn twenty-four hours a day.' He looked up at her at last. 'We can't live without the trees and the night sky, Nell. That's why we had to risk everything and take Gwen. But now at last I might see Duck again soon!'

She looked away, pretending there was something fascinating in the water. Anything but see his bruised face, and the light of hope in it. The things people did to each other were too bad to think about. Even her school had fights, where Jake and his friends would send out a challenge to the kids from the school on the next estate. They would all rush out when the bell went and charge through the streets until the two mobs met. If humans couldn't live together, how could they ever learn to live with another species, like the Elven?

'I remember the last time I saw Duck,' Evan said quietly. 'A Watcher was carrying her into the van. Her hair was sticking up and she was screaming. I don't even know what she looks like now.' He stood up. 'That's why we follow Fen, and do his bidding, Nell. He's all we've got, the only one who's on our side.'

She got to her feet too, and when she looked at him again, the bruises had gone. Now he just looked pale and tired.

Unlike the other Elven boy who came running out of the trees and leaped the rushing stream, a crossbow in his hand and quiver of arrows on his back.

'Wolves,' he shouted.

Faolan already knew. She was up on her feet, her legs like stilts. Her fur was bristling along her back.

They came out of the trees, brown, grey, brindle, fawn,

one almost black. They circled the clearing, moving like smoke. At their head was the arctic-white wolf with the pale ice-blue eyes. Thor.

'Fen needs to keep more control of them. They've been stalking both of us,' said the new boy, keeping his crossbow aimed at them.

She recognized him from the photos in Nan's study, the boy with the long hair and the bow and arrow aimed at the camera. He was wearing a camouflage top and combats, and he had two rabbits slung over his shoulder. A couple of ferrets played and chased round his feet like kittens.

'Stay still,' he warned. He threw the rabbits down on to the grass, then aimed. There was a hiss and the arrow streaked away from his bow and hit a tree inches away from Thor's white nose. The wolf yelped and disappeared into the trees. The others flowed after him.

'Nice shot,' said Evan. 'I didn't see them.'

The boy stowed his bow on his shoulder. 'They're getting worse, Evan. They're really cheeky now. Fen lets Thor get away with too much. They were tracking me, until they got a whiff of *her* scent.' He gave Nell a glance as though it was her fault she'd attracted the wolves' attention.

'This is Falcon,' Evan explained. 'He's our hunter.'

'Hey,' she said.

The boy looked unimpressed. 'So this is the human girl you were going on about?'

'Well spotted,' she said.

Falcon ignored her. He picked up the rabbits and walked across the clearing to a pile of flat smooth stones that had been balanced on each other to form something like a little shrine. One big stone was acting as a kind of table, and there were wilted bunches of flowers in jamjars and little bowls filled with what looked like nuts and berries.

He put one rabbit on top and took out a knife.

'What's he doing?' she whispered to Evan.

'We have to hunt to survive. But afterwards we have to ask Gaia's forgiveness for taking a life.'

She stared at the rabbits. 'That's what you eat?'

'Sometimes. When our parents were here, they worked the forest. It gave us all the food and drink we could want – venison, fruits, berries and fish from its streams. We dined like kings and queens. We took silver and gold from its rocks – Elven jewellery is the finest you'll ever see. It even provided our clothes – buckskin and leather, like your Native Americans.'

'Not now,' she said, looking at his hoodie. It was a make she knew, and it wasn't cheap.

He grinned. 'I never said we didn't come into the world and buy stuff as well. You know when you saw me in town, outside the jewellers'? I was selling our gold. We needed the money, because without the adults we can't live off the forest. We don't know how. Falcon does his best, and he's training up the younger ones, but it's hard for us.'

As they walked over, Falcon brought the knife down with a thud and a crunch. She saw him drip a little blood on to the stones. He said a few words, under his breath. They sounded like a prayer. Then he held out something to her. It was furry and bloody. He saw her face and laughed.

'Lucky rabbit's foot?' he taunted.

'No thanks.' She folded her arms. 'It wasn't very lucky for the rabbit.'

He was making her squirm on purpose, she could tell. Just like in Year 7 when she sat next to Ryan Burns in Biology, and he kept throwing dead frogs into her lap. Different species, same type of boy.

He put the lucky foot on the altar and slung the rabbits back over his shoulder. 'Good job we didn't pick her for the abduction,' he said. 'If she ended up staying here, she'd never survive.'

'Neither of them are staying here, it's all been sorted,'

said Evan quickly, but even he was smiling at her disgusted face as they left the clearing.

'Big deal,' she said. 'So I've got a thing about blood.'

'You can't have fears if you're Elven, Nell.' Evan led the way down another path. 'You're not tough enough for the forest life.'

'You think my life's easy,' she retorted. 'You've seen our school. All the mind games and the politics.'

He thought about that. Then nodded. 'You should try human school,' he said to Falcon, who was stalking along beside him. The boy looked horrified. 'It's trickier than a forest full of wolves.'

The two boys set a fast pace and after a few minutes Nell fell behind. When the other two were far ahead, she stopped and slipped the watch from her pocket and checked the position of the little sun. It was getting lower. Time was running out. How much farther had they to go? And how quickly could she find Gwen when she got to the palace?

She let her hands drag across a thorn bush growing at her side, then she ran after the other two. When she caught them up, Evan frowned and pointed to her hand.

'You're still bleeding,' he said.

Damn. She hadn't wanted him to notice the tiny drops of blood that were falling into the grass and pine needles. 'I got caught again. On a thorn.'

'Star will look at it when we get to the palace,' he said, as they strode on. 'She's training to be a healer, like old Lettie. She'll give you herbs and stuff to stop it going bad.'

'How long will that be?' she said, as they rounded yet another bend.

He stopped. 'Now.' He pointed along the path. 'We're here.'

Something huge and monstrous was blocking the way ahead, but it didn't resemble a building. All she could see was a wall of thorns amid the twisted roots of gigantic trees, and a jumble of rocks and logs that seemed to make a dam across the forest as high as she could see.

'Where?'

'It's right there,' he said, still pointing.

Then like a magic picture, her eyes adjusted and saw it.

Awful Fate Befalls Young Girl

Yesterday confirmed the worst fears of Mr J.W. Simmonds of Kibworth, that his daughter was indeed dead, on the discovery of her hat and cloak in woodland close to the Simmonds residence.

Lettice Simmonds, aged 15, disappeared two nights ago. On being interviewed her two older brothers fell to agonized weeping and Mr Simmonds looked careworn. 'What will we do without her?' he said.

Concerning certain remarks by some older Kibworth residents regarding a supposed fairy curse that claims young girls every hundred years, Mr Simmonds had this to say:

'Lettice was a shy girl, always modest in dress and manner, who wanted nothing more than to serve her father and brothers, as her mother had died when she was young. Earthly evil took my daughter, not faery.'

Kibworth Herald, 1913
Archives of the British Folklore Society
Edited by Druscilla Church

Fourteen

Someone had carved a sign on a circle of wood cut from a tree trunk. There were strange, spiky letters on it.

'Runes,' Evan said. 'It means "heart's desire".'

'It's amazing,' Nell breathed.

If a palace could be grown, then this was it. It looked three-quarters alive.

'You like it?'

She walked closer, tiptoeing as if the place might hear her and slam shut in her face. 'Absolutely. I don't like pretty things. I like awkward and faulty and prickly things.'

Evan stared at it. 'You came to the right place.'

'Heart's desire,' she said.

'It's what my mama called it.'

It looked liked Sleeping Beauty's thorn-covered castle, but darker. It was made of branches and stone and wood, with tree roots as the foundation. It towered above them, almost blotting out the little patches of sky she could see through the branches high above her.

'It wasn't always like this,' he said apologetically, as though she was a friend who'd been invited round for tea or a sleepover, and now he was worried that she might criticize the state of his home. 'It used to be less thorny, but after my parents were taken we let the forest grow around it, in case the Watchers ever get in. One day they might and then we really will be lost.'

As she got near she could see that the doorway was an arch between the giant roots of one massive central tree. Falcon had sat himself down near it, and was already skinning the rabbits. Trying not to look, Nell edged past him to follow Evan inside, but the boy put his foot out to stop her.

'She can't go through. She stinks of iron, Evan. You've got too used to being amongst humans.'

Nell found herself on the receiving end of a couple of enquiring charcoal stares, so she sighed and dug into the pocket of her leather jacket and took out the broken necklace. She dangled it from her fist.

'Is this what's bothering you?' she said.

Evan looked at it warily. 'Throw it away.'

'No, it's my sister's. I'll take it back when I go,' she

said, secretly crossing her fingers and praying she'd get back out.

There was a small lilac tree growing in a patch of sunlight near the doorway. It was in bloom and the heavy purple blossoms drooped down from the branches and scented the air all around. For some reason it had photos and drawings pinned to its trunk. They had a lilac tree in their garden at home, and sometimes her mum would break a bloom off and fix it to the dashboard of her car before she drove off. For a moment homesickness threatened to destroy her. Then she reached up on tiptoe and looped the necklace over the lowest branch. It tinkled prettily in the wind.

'Take it off,' snapped Falcon, standing up with the corpse of one rabbit dangling from his hand and tiny spots of blood on his white cheek. 'That's the memory tree.'

She took a longer look at the photos again. They were mainly family groups, all white-haired, all as beautiful as starlight. 'Are these the Elven who've been taken to the camps?'

Falcon nodded angrily.

'Well, my sister's been taken by *you*, so it can hang here.'

She stared as hard at Falcon as he was staring at her. She wouldn't look away. And for once she was the better starer. Gwen would have been proud.

Evan put a hand on Falcon's shoulder. 'Leave it, Fal. It's not for long.'

Reluctantly, the boy stood to one side, and she edged delicately past the bloody corpse and stalked into the stronghold. She stopped dead.

'Come on,' said Evan, moving ahead into the dimly lit passageway.

The darkness sucked at her mind. She could see passages leading in all directions, dark and winding, like something a minotaur would charge through. Her hair began to stand on end.

I wish I hadn't thought about monsters.

She felt like one of the forest creatures, the smaller fluffier ones, not the wolves and stags, the ones whose lives were ruled by the fear of predators leaping out at them 24/7, so their nerves were always jangling.

Something was trailing her in the darkness. It was worse than the feeling of being watched in the forest. It was something dangerous. Something that buzzed like a million angry killer bees.

She wanted to flee back outside, but time was running out. She had to locate Gwen and get her out. She felt her skin go cold and clammy. For a moment she thought she was about to have a panic attack. She'd had two before and they were terrifying; all the gasping for breath and the feeling you were going to die and that the world might come crashing down on your head. No, she couldn't freak out now she'd come this far. She was Gwen's last hope.

She took a packet of gum from her pocket and ate a piece. The taste of green apples burst in her mouth. She inhaled the smell and it was as though Gwen was there next to her.

Straight away something tapped her arm. She looked down into the eyes of two little girls. They were holding out their hands like Oliver Twist. They'd really worked hard on looking cute and adorable.

'Can we have some bubbly, human girl?' said the one with white bunches.

'We're starving,' chirped the other, who looked like a white-haired, black-eyed kitten. 'We're just little Elvlings. We haven't got any sweeties.'

Nell glanced at Evan, who was shaking his head at the girls and trying to shoo them away.

'We can do fairy magic!' said the first. 'We'd do some for you.'

'You can't do magic,' said Evan. 'Now scram!'

The two little faces changed, and went sharp like meerkats.

'Can.'

'We don't like you now, Evan.'

Evan gave a pretend growl at them. That got him a couple of scowls.

'Not fair.'

'We want bubbly.'

'Here. Have some,' said Nell, getting the packet out again.

Immediately the two girls switched back to being adorable. 'We love you, human girl!' they sang, holding out their hands.

She threw them a couple of pieces. One girl caught both and for a moment there was a scrap, like a ball of fighting kittens. They even curled up their mouths and hissed at each other like kittens. So Evan got one in one hand and one in the other.

'Pixie, Fay, go, leave us alone.'

This time they went, skipping into the darkness, cheeking Evan all the way.

'Oh my God, they're so sweet,' said Nell. They seemed to have broken the spell on her, too. Whatever had been watching wasn't there any more. 'I don't expect the forest can supply bubble-gum.'

'No. It's like gold dust round here. You'll see, the little ones will do anything for it.'

Chewing on her gum, she followed him down a

passageway that had walls woven out of live branches like an organic tapestry, but something else was nagging at her mind. It took her a while to realize what. It was too quiet in here. She couldn't hear the sound of hysterics echoing down the passages, no one screaming, no one shouting, no one weeping loudly or swearing at the top of their voice.

She couldn't hear Gwen.

'Where's my sister,' she said urgently, as the darkness sucked at her mind again and in the distance the bees buzzed. What if this was a trick? What if Gwen wasn't here? Her heart started to flutter.

'I'm taking you to her now,' Evan said. Then, with a frown, as if he'd read her mind, 'You know I would never trick you.'

She nodded and followed him. What choice did she have?

Now she was in the hall.

This was where the Elven lived their lives, he told her. It was large and stone-walled. Music played. Even though it was daylight outside, it was dark in here, except for the great spears of sunlight lancing down from high above. Round the sides, lanterns had been been lit and hung from branches. A huge roaring fire on a big bed of ashes crackled and smoked in the centre of the room. The smoke spiralled up and out of a hole in the roof, which was more like a canopy of leaves than a proper ceiling. The flames were mottling the tiled floor and lighting the faces of the children who were lounging around.

More Elven. She caught her breath. Maybe these were the ones she'd seen flitting amongst the trees last night.

'All Rivers?' she whispered.

'Cousins. And cousins of cousins. And cousins of cousins of—'

'I get it.'

None of them looked older than her or Evan. Everything about them glittered, from their hair to the silver and gold at their throats, ears and wrists. There was a quicksilver quality about their movements too, as though she might turn round, turn back and they would all be gone.

Some were sitting at a long wooden table over to one side, where a cluster of breakfast cereals from her world stood in the middle. Some were sitting on sofas and piles of cushions around the fire, listening to their iPods, or doing each other's hair, or lying back and playing with handheld consoles.

Her nan had said they only *looked* human, but it seemed to Nell that they were not so different. They were

playing games like she did. They were determined to ruin their teeth by eating Sugar Puffs and Coco Pops, like she and Gwen did. And when Evan led her into the centre of the room, and twenty pairs of eyes, charcoal, slanting, full of trickiness, stared at her as if she was some sort of exotic creature – they were acting exactly how Gwen's gang did when someone new was sighted. Hands went to mouths, the whispering began and the staring turned to sly glances.

She stayed close to Evan. Would he pretend he hardly knew her now, in front of the Elven? What if she told them they used to sit and have lunch together?

'Watch her, she kicks,' was the only introduction he gave her.

A couple of the girls came skipping over to him, but when they saw Nell, they tossed back their long hair and walked away again, their eyes full of icy mistrust. Usually she would have felt hurt, but now there wasn't time. No time for worrying about what they thought of her, or if she was going to say the right thing. There was now, this moment, that was all.

'They don't like me,' she said.

Evan nodded. 'True. But no one will hurt you, Nell. We aren't angels. But nor are humans.'

The only one grinning delightedly at her was Bean, the

little boy who'd been riding on the Vespa with Evan. He trundled up on a brightly coloured pushalong and babbled something to her.

'Bean is Falcon's brother,' he said, trying to wipe chocolate from round the little boy's mouth. 'The Watchers took their parents, but Falcon managed to escape with Bean. He can't even remember his mama now.'

Bean babbled something else.

Evan translated. 'He saw you with long hair. He wants to know where it's gone.'

'That was the old me. Before I met the Elven,' she told Bean. 'This is the new me.'

She reached into her pocket to get him some gum, but she didn't get the chance. A girl with her long platinum hair hanging like a waterfall down her back flounced over and picked the little boy up, protectively, as though he was in danger of being attacked by the nasty human girl.

'It's OK, Lily, she's with me,' said Evan. 'Everything's going to be all right.'

The girl hugged Bean closer, but she stopped looking so unfriendly. Nell rustled up a smile for her then followed Evan across to the fire.

'If there's no adults, who looks after you?' she said.

He pulled a face. 'It's mainly me,' he admitted. 'I

have to see that they're all safe. I have to see that they eat fruit sometimes. I have to make them go to sleep before midnight.'

As if to prove a point a small boy trotted over to him and said, 'I broke 'em again,' and handed him a pair of glasses with one hand and the lenses with the other. She watched as Evan took a small screwdriver from his pocket and began to fix the lenses back in. It looked like he'd done this many times.

'But you're fourteen,' she said.

The shrug again. 'There's no one else, Nell.' He handed the mended glasses back to the boy, who put them on and then skipped away. Then he clapped his hands to get everyone's attention. 'What's up with you all?' he shouted. 'Where's our famous Elven hospitality? We've got a guest.' He delved into a box next to a rack of blackened pots and pans.

'Do you want something to eat?' he said. 'It's a long way back through the forest.'

She shook her head. 'My nan told me stories about fairy food. Once you accept it you're in their power.'

Evan held up a big packet of tortilla chips. 'I don't think Tesco's do an enchanted range. I told you, we don't always eat berries and hunt rabbits.'

She eyed the bag. Yes, she wanted to tell him. She

would love to sit here and talk and eat tortilla chips and dip. Anything to stop her thinking about what she would soon have to do. But she couldn't.

'No,' she said. 'I want to see Gwen.'

She didn't get to say any more because suddenly the peace of the hall was split by hissing and snarling. She turned round expecting to see a dog and cat fighting, but it was two Elven, a boy and a girl.

'Sky, Crystal – stop,' said Evan without turning round.

There was a pause. 'He ate the last cookie!' howled the girl. 'It was mine.' She wrinkled her nose and hissed at him, just like a cat. He curled his lip and snarled back. 'Mine!'

'Mine!'

'Gdask!'

'F'rshak!'

'So girl Elven hiss, and boy Elven snarl?' she said to Evan as the children continued to spit insults at each other.

'Pretty much.'

'Dogbreath,' hissed the little girl.

This time Evan whirled round. 'Stop, both of you. Go pick some fruit outside if you're hungry.'

'We can't. Fen's outside with Thor,' said the boy. 'He's being mean. We're scared of him. He's looking for you and he's mad.'

Nell's blood ran cold. If he was mad at his own brother, what would he do to her?

'Has he got Gwen with him?' she whispered.

'Stop worrying, I know where she is.' He began to walk away.

She grabbed his sleeve. 'Tell me. I'll go to her.'

He pulled away. 'No. First I'll go and calm Fen down. Promise I won't be long,' he said, over his shoulder. 'Star – see to her cuts!'

'No!'

Too late, he was out the door. Great. Would this never end? Would she never get to see her sister?

She wrapped her arms around herself and stared at the fire. At least that meant she didn't have to see all the Elven watching her.

'Hmm, perhaps human girls ought to be more careful,' said a sweet but unfriendly voice.

She turned around. It was the Elven girl she'd seen in the photo at Nan's, the one with long hair in intricate little plaits, who'd stalked her through the mist like a ghost, last night. She didn't look like a ghost now. She was sitting cross-legged next to the fire, on a long wooden bench that had been heaped with quilts and cushions. She was all in white, with a line of little rune tattoos running across her

199

thin arm. Silver earrings made up of moons and stars dangled from her ears and silver chains sparkled on her wrists and throat. She was crushing dried berries and herbs with a mortar and pestle. A wooden box was open in front of her, full of little bottles and jars.

Nell thought she'd never seen anyone so pretty. If she'd unfolded a pair of fairy wings there and then, she wouldn't have been surprised.

'You're a bit younger than I expected.'

Two small lines appeared between Star's eyebrows. 'So? All the other doctors got taken by the Watchers. And I *am* studying hard.'

She put the mortar and pestle down with a slight bang.

'I know the language of flowers. I know the thousand basic herbs and where to find them. I can make decoctions and potions – if someone helps me lift the big copper cauldron.' She took a bottle from the box and shook it, then blinked at Nell. 'So I think I can deal with a few scratches.'

'Sorry. I didn't mean anything,' said Nell quickly. 'Don't worry about the scratches. I haven't time.'

Star ignored her.

'*And* I can blend the ten base elements which is amazing at my age.' She peered at Nell's hand, wrinkling her nose. 'But only if Lettie's here, because I'm not allowed to use fire on my own.'

Something stirred in Nell's memory. 'Lettie?'

The mountain of quilts piled on the end of the couch moved and revealed themselves to be covering a little old lady.

'That's me, duckie,' she said. Her hair was wispy and white like all the Elven, but instead of charcoal her eyes were milky blue, and her skin was as brown and wrinkled as an old apple.

Nell felt her mouth drop open in astonishment as she remembered where she'd heard a similar name.

'You're not from here,' she breathed. 'You're Lettice. The Victorian girl who was kidnapped.'

'That's right!'

'I read about you in my nan's book.'

The old lady seemed weirdly happy, but ice ran down Nell's spine. This would be Gwen's fate if she didn't manage to rescue her. In a hundred years' time she'd be like this, a little old lady who'd wasted her whole life, imprisoned in a land that wasn't hers.

And you, you'll be like that, too, if you don't get a move on! whispered Helene spitefully.

'Long time since I saw a human, dear.'

'I bet. You've been a hostage all your life,' Nell

said sympathetically. But this only made Lettie cackle, gleefully.

'I was never kidnapped!' she exclaimed. 'Half the girls weren't. You should tell your grandmother – I wanted to come here.' She shook her wispy little head. 'The nights I stood and waited! The searching I had to do to find a mist.'

Nell frowned. 'You wanted to be abducted?' she said slowly.

Lettie's old face crinkled up into a roguish smile. 'I'd met an Elven boy, you see. And I wanted to go. We waited for a stormy night, just for the look of things, and then me and my boy danced through the mist.' Her smile became triumphant. 'I never missed any of my family. Especially Father. He deserved it.' The old woman's withered hand patted Nell's arm. 'Mother had died when I was young, and because I was the only girl I had to do all the housework and cook the meals for *him* and my brothers. He took me out of school, no one bothered back then. That was to be my life, but I wanted more.' She looked around. 'And I got it, I'm pleased to say.'

'But you must be over a hundred now,' said Nell, awestruck.

'We live a long time in the forest.'

'Because of the pure air and lack of pollution?'

Lettie gave a thin, cackling laugh. 'No, duckie, because life's so exciting with the Elven. The travel, the parties, the excitement! And if I had my time over again, I'd do exactly the same. In my day girls got to do hardly anything. Here, I've been . . .' she ticked them off on her fingers, '. . . a hunter, a warrior, a healer, a matchmaker and a queen.'

'A queen? But you're not Elven.'

'Girls who cross over and come to live here are counted as Elven.' She smiled, modestly. 'I was a good queen, until I got fed up with it. The Elven kings and queens are like the leaders of a wolf pack. They're allowed to rule, just as long as they do their job well. If they don't do it, then they get replaced. Simple. No respect, no job.' She chuckled. 'Our present king – Fen and Evan's father – what a man he is! He could make a wolf stop attacking and hand over its teeth!' She cackled gently to herself. 'You should be glad you're here. This is the place to be.'

'No!' This was wrong. Nothing would make Gwen's abduction right. 'Some of those girls didn't want to come here. Some of them would have pined for their families.'

Lettie leaned back and pulled the quilts around her again. 'Tell that to the Elven and you know what would happen? They would look at you in surprise and say they were doing it to help the girls. That their life here is so much better than in the human world. They saw it as freeing the girls. They think they're blessed.'

Before Nell could answer, Star grabbed her hand and dabbed something on it that stung like a wasp.

'Hope that didn't hurt, human girl,' she said, in a not very innocent voice.

Oh, so that's your game, thought Nell. She hid a wince and gave Star a little smile instead. The Elven looked surprised.

'OK, try this,' she said brightly. She took a few leaves from one of the jars, chewed them for a moment or two and then spat them on to her hand. She pressed the green mush on to Nell's biggest scratch. Nell never flinched.

Star said, 'Huh,' then got something else out of another jar.

'What's that, a dried slug?' said Nell, as casually as she could. It did actually look like one, but she was determined not to let Star know she hated slugs and worms.

Star shook her head. She unrolled the dark tube and then spread the delicate fabric over the wound. 'No, caterpillar skin.'

Ew, ew, ew, said Nell silently. But she kept her face straight. 'Fine.'

Star's eyebrows rose. She looked mildly impressed. It seemed Nell had passed some sort of test.

'Not bad for a human girl,' she said, packing away some of the jars. 'Pity you weren't the one who got kidnapped.'

Nell froze. She could handle the caterpillar skin, but she wasn't going to take that.

'No one should have been kidnapped!' she said. 'That's why Gwen will be freed. She's going back to the human world!'

There were gasps from all around. Nell hadn't realized the Elven were listening. Some of them clapped their hands excitedly.

'She is? Then it worked!' one cried. 'The Watchers are going to open the camps. Fen's plan worked.'

And that's all it took to change the atmosphere in the room. Suddenly Nell found herself at the centre of attention. The Elven girls and boys sitting nearby came over, then others joined them. At first they still gave her wary looks and kept their distance, but their faces were changing from sharp and foxy to something much friendlier.

Only Star watched silently, sucking the end of one of her little plaits.

One of the young girls grabbed Nell's hands excitedly. 'We like you now, human girl.'

And as the other Elven smiled at her, it was as though

the world had gone from black and white to colour. She was dazzled. So this was why the Elven had been loved in ancient times, she thought. When they were happy there was a magic about them. They were like celebrities, they shone and sparkled. If only she wasn't running out of time and sick with worry, because she was lying to them, it would've been amazing.

'We never liked a human before!'

'We were worried about the kidnap,' confessed another, after looking around to see who was listening. 'But Fen said it would work. Now we'll get our parents back.'

'We thought humans hated us and wanted us dead.'

'We never spoke to one before.'

'You go to the cinema,' said Nell, as they bounced around her. 'You have to ask for seats.'

'They mean we don't make friends,' said Star, packing away her medicine box. 'We don't connect.'

She met Star's eyes. 'Maybe you should. We're not that different.'

Star gave her a thoughtful look, then someone else tapped her arm. 'Have you met Fen yet?'

The mention of Fen's name made them all go quiet.

'No, just Evan,' she said. Where was he? She looked towards the door, willing him to come back.

'He's training me to be a warrior,' said one of the older

boys. He was wearing camo gear.

'We're all in awe of him,' said the boy next to him, who was dressed identically as though they were in a private army. 'He's going to save us all.'

Nell frowned. 'Who? Evan?'

'No!' The two boys looked at each other. They held out their wrists to her. She saw the two little tattoos. 'Fen of course. He's the wolf.'

'Oh,' said Nell. 'I'd follow Evan if I were you.'

Star leaned close to her. 'For a human you see things clearly,' she whispered grudgingly. 'Be careful. Something's wrong with Fen. He has a shadow in his eye.'

'Yes. I saw it in photos of him,' said Nell. 'One eye glows, the other doesn't.'

Star nodded. 'I have worked out the fifteen crucial herbs for removing it, but none of us can get near him.' She hesitated, as though it was against her better judgement to open her heart to a human. 'When you meet him, don't make him angry. The shadow is in his mind as well.' Then she carried on packing up her medicine box as though she'd never spoken.

From the bundle of quilts, Lettie's old hand reached out and grasped hers. 'You be careful, duckie,' she croaked. 'She's right. Fen has the darkness in him. He's crazy in the head.'

'No, he's not. He's a freedom fighter. He's a warrior,' said one of the boys. 'He's doing it for us.'

The old lady's finger poked at him. 'He's mad and bad, I tell you!'

The Elven looked at each other, and then started laughing and shouting again. But Nell could hear something in their voices. Underneath the excitement they sounded desperate and a little scared. Join the club, she thought. Her hand went to the moon watch in her pocket. She could feel the *tick*, *tick*, *tick* as the little sun moved ever closer to the cloud.

Time, it was all down to time! Evan had told her they were outside time here. But go through the mist any later than sunset and a whole lot of time would hit Gwen and she'd wither in an instant into old age.

She *had* to make it back.

'Stop!' she said loudly. 'Where's Evan?'

'I'm here.'

He was behind her, running a hand through his hair, making it spiky, and trying not to look worried.

Star gave him a look. Evan replied with a shrug. 'I couldn't find him. He's lurking somewhere.'

'Try his lair,' she whispered. 'Watch out. He's banging his head and raging. He's getting worse.'

Nell tugged his sleeve. 'I must see Gwen, now,'

she said urgently.

He nodded. 'Can you climb?'

She looked down at her muddy feet. 'Let me check – have I got my heels on today?'

He went to laugh but then stopped himself. 'A word of warning. Don't try any of your jokes on Fen.'

The main stairs for the palace were carved out of the trunk of the massive tree that ran through the centre of the structure. It went up and up as far as she could see.

Every now and then they would come to balconies that looked out on to the forest. There were little clusters of Elven on these, playing games or making things out of sticks and twigs. She saw two little girls skipping to something that sounded suspiciously like an Elven version of 'I like coffee, I like tea', that she and Gwen used to sing. On the next floor a group of boys were practising firing arrows over the balcony. Next to them were two girls who seemed to be looking after a whole zoo of small, furry creatures. On another a boy stood on his own, staring out over the forest with one of the enormous lammergeyers perched on his arm.

As they climbed past, some of the Elven ran up to Evan and said things like, 'Tell Storm! She won't let me have her bow,' or, 'Evan, come and see what we've made, come on, you must!' Or they would wind themselves round his legs like he was their favourite brother, and he'd have to stop and unpeel them and tell them that he'd see them later.

Even though she was desperate to see Gwen, she couldn't help stopping and watching him as he tended to them. He's different, she thought. That's why I liked him.

Most people wanted control. Gwen controlled everyone with cold shoulders and rules. Church had his badge and his men. Fen blacked the town out and held people to ransom. But Evan did something else. He looked after all the ones who'd got left behind. He kept them together and kept them free. He was the prince of small things, and she wanted to hug him for it.

They climbed on, higher and higher. Evan fell silent. With each step his face was becoming more and more strained. Her knees began to feel like jelly and not just because of the endless stairs. She stopped for a breather as they passed another balcony. They'd climbed so high she could see far out over the forest, as it stretched endlessly in all directions. In the distance she could make out some of the towering harps, shrunk to the size of needles.

A moment later she heard him shout, 'Come on! You're nearly at the top.'

She ran up one last curve of the stairs on to a wide open platform, supported by the massive branches of the tall central tree. He was waiting for her and he held out his hand and pulled her up the last step. He didn't let go for a moment.

'This is Fen's lair. I can't help you here,' he said quietly. 'He's beyond listening to me. So watch yourself, Nell.'

Did he look scared? She couldn't tell, but she began to shiver.

Above them the sky had the same strange, twisted look as the night sky. It was a bright, cold blue lit by a dazzling sun. A flimsy-looking guardrail, made from planks of wood, was all that protected them from the drop to the forest below. She looked down over the edge. It was like being on the deck of a ship, sailing above a very green sea. A warship, because Fen had fixed guns and rifles around the railings. He'd also been busier than Falcon when it came to hunting the forest creatures. There were bones all over the decking, gnawed by wolves. The skins of rabbits and other creatures had been pegged along the rail to dry in the sun, and there was a pile of furs laid out in one corner.

Gwen would freak. She hated heights. She hated icky things like bloody skins. So why couldn't she hear her screaming?

'Gwen?' she called.

'She won't answer, she's asleep,' said Evan. He pointed to the heap of furs.

Nell ran over. Gwen was lying curled up with her wonderful hair spread out like a fan and a bloodstained bandage around her neck. She looked like the Lady of Shalott, ready to float down the river. She looked like Sleeping Beauty, or Snow White, waiting for her prince.

Of course she did, thought Nell, as she took her sister's limp hand. Anyone else would have red eyes, matted hair and a runny nose, but no, Gwen just looked hauntingly beautiful and sad.

She'd made it. Here was her sister, still breathing. She crouched on the floor.

'Wake up,' she whispered.

'She can't hear you,' said Evan, from behind her.

'What have you done to her?' she said urgently. 'Did you give her drugs?'

'No. Fen hexed her.' He held up his hands, as Nell jumped angrily to her feet. 'It's not dangerous. It's an enchanted sleep. She's dreaming that she's still at her sweet sixteen party. She'll remember nothing when she goes back to your world.'

But that didn't help Nell. How could she abduct her own sister if she was fast asleep?

'Wake her up,' she said, patting Gwen's face and trying to get some reaction from her. But there was nothing.

'I can't. Fen says she's to stay asleep.'

Nell wanted to scream.

'Time's running out,' she said. 'You have to wake her. We can't take her to meet Church if she's asleep!'

'I know. But he has to do it.'

She spun round. 'OK, where is he?'

He had no time to answer. Someone was storming up the stairs, someone who brought the sound of angry bees with them. The buzzing blew across the battlements towards her and hit her in the stomach, almost winding her. She braced herself. Her hands grabbed for the rail.

It was Fen, coming for her.

Fifteen

Nell wanted to fall to her knees and clap her hands against her ears. She wanted to run from the sound before it drilled into her head and drove her mad.

Her martial arts teacher said that some people had more chi than others, a life force that you could feel like a strong wind hitting you in the stomach. Fen had powerful chi, but it was all over the place. She could feel chaos streaming from him.

He emerged out of the shadows and stalked towards her, frighteningly tall. She wanted to back away but she glued her feet to the floor. She'd seen him as a shadow in the woods, now here he was, with the sunshine washing over him and etching him in gold. He looked as though he could star on the cover of a magazine about badass but cool people.

'Beautiful as starlight, fierce as wolves, cold as ice,' she murmured.

'Yeah, some of us got more of the starlight than others,' said Evan, at her shoulder, in something more like his old voice.

'I was thinking he'd got more of the ice.'

Gwen would certainly have fallen for him if she'd been awake. But it was a cruel kind of handsomeness. His eyes were all black, like a Staffie's. There were dark shadows around them, as though he'd been ill. And when he came closer she could see that his skin wasn't like Evan's, translucent like porcelain, but chalk white. Thor was at his heels, his ice-blue eyes pinned on her. They were alike, the wolf and the Elven, both predators, smiling the special smile of those who know their prey is already under their paws.

'Who's she?' he said, baring sharp white teeth, like Thor's. 'You picked up a human girl?'

'What, like you do?' said Nell, before she could stop herself. Out of the corner of her eye, she saw Evan give her a warning look.

'Cheeky too,' said Fen. 'You'd better tell her to watch her mouth.'

Evan shifted his feet uncomfortably. 'Stop it, Fen. She's Gwen's little sister.'

He lifted an eyebrow. 'Ah, this is the one I wasn't to

kidnap. Well, little brother, she's all yours . . .' he gave a grin, '. . . later. First I need her.'

'What's that supposed to mean?' said Nell.

'It means I've now got myself two hostages.' He licked his lips. 'Double the fun. Double the pain for Church.'

'No!' Nell backed away, but Fen gave a brief whistle through his teeth and Thor was there, at her back. She could feel the wolf's hot breath on her legs, his jowls pulled back in a snarl, ready to bite.

'You're quieter than her at any rate. I had to hex your sister before she deafened me with her screams.'

'Stop it,' pleaded Evan. 'Nell's here with good news. The Watchers are going to let the Elven go free. First we have to give Gwen back.'

'Do we?' said Fen. 'Maybe I've changed my mind.'

He started circling Nell, trailed by Thor.

'You can't do that,' she said, turning on her heel to keep them both in sight.

Fen laughed unpleasantly. 'Do you realize how powerful I am? Your grandmother's insane to think she can beat me.'

No, it's you that's insane, thought Nell.

For a moment he stopped and winced as though a sudden pain had shot through his eye. He rubbed it. He shook his head, cursing, then banged his eye socket hard with the heel of his hand, and roared like a bull in distress. Both she and Evan stepped back. It was like being close to an injured wild animal. He was so unpredictable.

'Fen – you OK?' said Evan.

'Shut up!' Fen howled. 'My head hurts. I don't need you whining all the time.'

He blinked and seemed to get his focus back. It was all on Nell. He clicked his fingers in her face and a spark leaped between them.

'I'm not going to bring Ragnarok, I am Ragnarok. I can control electricity now. I can store it up, block it off, make it flow where I want – like magic. Your leaders are right to be scared of us. We only wanted to share with you. Now we could rule the world – or wipe you out.'

He began circling again. Nell swung round, keeping him in sight. 'Big deal. Anyone with a massive enough bomb could do that, but somehow they don't.'

He wasn't listening. She had a feeling that he'd not listened to anyone for ages.

'I'm like one of the Vanir!' he gloated. 'Like a god from the old days.'

She glanced at Evan. He was rooted to the spot, staring at Fen, his eyes wide like a kid who's seen something terrible.

'I heard you telling the story of the Elf-King who was

robbed of his child,' Fen said. 'Now I'm the Elf-King.'

There was a noise from Evan, a sort of choke. 'You're not the king, Dad still is. You can't take over, that's not how it works. You have to be elected.'

Fen swung round on his brother. 'I *am* the king,' he said savagely. Then he was back to circling Nell. His finger jabbed out at her. 'You've robbed us of the world. Now I'm going to get it back. I'll save the Elven.'

Nell kept her eyes on him. 'Seems to me that it's Evan saving the Elven, not you.'

A corner of his mouth lifted, like a wolf. 'Wiping Bean's nose is not saving anyone.'

'You just want war. You're as bad as the humans who want you gone.'

He turned around and drew his fist back and aimed at her. Nell squeezed her eyes shut and waited for the pain. There was a loud crack. She opened her eyes. His fist had struck a wooden post an inch from her face.

She heard Evan draw a ragged breath, but Fen burst out laughing.

'Don't worry. I wouldn't hit that pretty human face. You're not a patch on your sister, though. She's the honey.'

'If you want to make me jealous of Gwen, don't bother,' she said coolly. 'Old news. And anyway, Paige and Bria are so much better at it. It's a girl thing.'

He punched the wall again, even closer to her face. 'And that's a boy's answer.'

'It's a bully's answer,' she muttered.

'Nell, please shut up,' said Evan breathlessly.

'Why?' she said. 'I never did anything to hurt anyone. I'm too young. So why's he taking it out on me?'

'This is my lair,' Fen said. 'You don't get to cheek me.'

He grabbed her and dragged her across the deck and threw her against the flimsy railings. The dizzying drop was inches from her feet.

'Did Evan blab? Did he tell you that our land is dying?'

In the corner of her eye she could see Evan, frozen in the act of stepping towards her, his hands out as though trying to think of some way to rescue her. Then Fen put his hand on the back of her neck, forcing her to look out over the forest. He jabbed a finger towards the horizon.

'See far over there? That's where the winter lake lies. And in the centre is the Mother Harp that makes all the others sing.'

She squinted at the distant horizon. A dark cloud was spread along it as though someone had drawn a line across the sky in indigo paint. It looked like the start of a spreading bruise.

'The song is fading. The land is starting to untwist itself. And we're getting storms. They come in the afternoons, before sunset, out of the darkness of the lake.' He pointed to the growing stain in the sky. 'That's one of them, heading our way.'

Nell's heart sank. Not only did she have to rescue Gwen, but get her back through the forest during a storm.

'Can't you feel it?' Fen said. For a moment her head swam and she felt dizzy. 'That's the pressure dropping,' he explained. He sniffed the air like a wolf. 'It's going to be a big one today.'

'Fen, listen to me,' said Evan desperately, walking closer with his hands up as though to show his brother he meant no harm. 'The Watchers have agreed. We take Gwen to the mist, and we do the swap. They're opening the camps and setting the Elven free.'

Fen gave a mocking laugh. He let Nell go and took hold of his brother's shirt and pulled him close. He stared for a moment or two, then ruffled his hair as though he was three years old.

'Brother,' he said, letting the disappointment show in his voice. 'When are you going to get wise? You've been fooled by a human. She's lying.' He turned his head and gave Nell a quick snarl. 'There's no agreement by the Watchers. How could there be?'

Evan shook his head. 'You're wrong.'

'No!' Fen punched him on the arm, viciously. 'She's lying.'

Evan winced but made no sound. He looked at Nell.

'He's wrong, isn't he?' he said, through gritted teeth. 'Tell him!'

She couldn't speak. She couldn't look at him. She felt as though the floor had given way beneath her.

'Nell, tell him it's true!'

She forced herself to look squarely back at him. 'Of course it's true. Nan promised. Fen's wrong.'

But her voice had trembled and now he was staring at her, shocked. He shook his head.

'He's not,' he said slowly, as the truth dawned. 'I know your face, Nell. He's right. You're lying.'

'No, I—' she began helplessly, hardly knowing what to say.

'But I trusted you.'

'Trusted a human!' Fen gave a triumphant laugh, like a cock crowing. Evan cursed and swung round at him.

'Shut up! You knew when you took Gwen that it wouldn't work! All along you meant to keep her. Why?'

Fen's lip curled again. 'Hurt. That's what I want to

cause her family. Like the hurt that's been done to ours.'
He shoved Evan away roughly, then turned to Nell. 'Now
you get hexed too. That'll shut you up.'

The noise of bees started up again, worse than
before. This was like a million killer bees, all angry,
buzzing round inside her head, until she thought it would
burst. She clapped her hands over her ears, but it made
no difference.

'Please, stop!' she cried.

Over the terrible noise she heard Evan shout, 'Leave
it, Fen!'

Then his brother was going for him again. 'Learn!'
he shouted. 'Learn to be strong like me. Remember we
hate the humans.'

Evan went into a crouch, his eyes blazing. She saw his
top lip curl up, and then he was snarling and hissing at
his brother. Fen crouched and snarled back. They were
like a wolf and a cub having a stand-off.

'You knew the Watchers wouldn't agree,' Evan
growled. 'Why did you lie to me?'

Fen hissed back, and for a few seconds they circled
each other. Then Fen made one quick movement and
Evan was spinning back against the flimsy barrier,
cracking it and sliding over the edge.

Nell screamed. At the last moment his hand grasped

the broken fence, then his other hand caught hold. Fen didn't even bother to check if he was OK. He turned back to her and began to drone words. It sounded like something a bee would say if it knew how to talk. Was this the Elven language, or something magical? She tried to listen, to concentrate. But there was an edge of fuzzy black growing around her vision. The world began to sway and retreat into the distance. She was going to faint.

'No!' She clapped her hands over her ears. 'Stop.' Her knees began to shake.

If he hexed her, they were here for good. She and Gwen would be stuck in a land that couldn't last.

Lettie chose to stay, because she hated her life, Nell thought wildly. But I like mine. I do. I used to think it sucked, but I like it. I want to disrespect Gwen's gang again. I want to see Bria's mouth drop open and Paige go all gormless just because I answered back. I want to walk around knowing they've got no power to hurt me, none at all. They're like tissue paper enemies. I can blow them away with one big breath. I want to go and sit on their lunch table and take up space and not move when they tell me to, and perhaps invite a couple more unfavourites and losers to sit with me.

As her eyes blurred, she saw Evan clamber back up. He

was looking from her to Fen in horror. She felt her legs go like rubber bands, but she fought it for a moment or two. Then something went clunk in her head. Blackness swarmed across her eyes, and the last thing she remembered was Evan's hands reaching out and catching her as she fell forward into the darkness.

Sixteen

Nell's cheek was against something soft. It felt like sheepskin. It was comforting, like being a baby again and wrapped up warm, but it didn't stop her head aching. It was like last Christmas when Gwen spiked her Coke with vodka and she'd had to be helped to bed. She lay still until the thumping died down.

'Gsak, ma'forshlan orl kana. Gsak, ma'forshlan orl kana.'

Someone was whispering. She kept her eyes closed. Whatever it was, it sounded like the words Fen had used to put her to sleep, but these were being said gently, not in a temper. And it wasn't Fen's voice, it was Evan's.

He was bringing her out of the hex.

She listened carefully. It was one line repeated over and over, strange words that sounded as if you were

227

chewing razor blades. She let them sink into her half-waking mind.

The voice stopped. 'I know you're awake.'

She kept still.

'And you've been awake for the last three times I said the release spell,' he continued flatly. 'Does your mama have this trouble in the mornings?'

'Yes.'

Nell opened her eyes. The world consisted of the twisted sky and Evan's face. If she thought he was pale before, his face was snow white now. She held on to her head and sat up. She was still on the high platform above the forest. Gwen was lying on the furs, doing her Sleeping Beauty impersonation.

'Sorry,' she said. 'For tricking you.'

His eyes were cold. 'You're always sorry.'

'You would've lied to rescue Bean or Star from us.'

'Yes, I would have. It's what Elven do. We lie to humans. But I thought me and you were different.'

He turned away and she saw a swelling lump on the side of his cheekbone. It already had a hint of blue and green.

'Ouch. Did Fen hit you?'

He put a hand up to the bruise. 'It doesn't matter,' he said briefly. Then he gave an exasperated groan and said, 'I don't get it, Nell. You lied to me to get to Gwen – and then what? You were going to steal her and flee back to the mist?'

'Yes.'

'That's insane.'

'Pretty much.'

He threw out his hands in despair. 'Why did you have to be so brave? Why couldn't you accept that some things have to happen?' He leaped to his feet.

She scrambled after him. 'Where's Fen?'

'He's gone off with Thor.' He started towards the staircase. 'You've got to run. I'll get you back to the mist. We'll flit.'

She forgot about her headache as relief washed over her. So there was still time. 'Thanks! Wake Gwen and we'll go.'

He came back to her.

'No. Not Gwen. You,' he said.

Nell gaped at him in horror. 'But I can't leave without my sister, Evan.'

He grabbed her hand. 'It's that or nothing. He'll be back soon.' His grip got stronger. 'Trust me. You don't have much time. It's too late for Gwen.'

'No, it's not dark yet.' She pulled her hand away. 'You have no right to keep her!'

229

'You've seen Fen. You've seen how he's acting,' he said roughly. 'What choice do I have?'

He turned away angrily, stalked over to the railing and stared out over the forest. He was right, it was getting late. The sun had gone in and the purple bruise of the storm was covering half the sky and rushing towards them so fast she could see it eating up the blue.

She went and stood beside him, their hair blowing in the sudden cold wind. Where their hands rested on the rails, little sparks of static zipped and fizzed. There was thunder and lightning in the air.

'I know you hate me now, but please!' she said, through gritted teeth. 'You have to help get us both out.'

He shook his head. 'I have to keep the others safe. Fen would go mad if I took Gwen back. I don't know what he'd do, if he thought we'd betrayed him.'

'He's paranoid.'

Evan gave a choked laugh. 'We're all paranoid. One way we've got the storms, the other way there's the humans and the Watchers. We're stuck and we're scared.'

Nell turned her back to the storm, so she couldn't see it approaching. 'That's not Gwen's fault.'

Evan shrugged. Little sparks lit up his hair. 'He never used to be like this, Nell. He was my big brother, he looked after me. I thought he was amazing. Then when our parents got taken he changed. He couldn't sleep. I used to hear him walking about all night long, pacing up and down, muttering to himself. Then he started saying he sensed the storms coming and moved up here to the battlements. He said they spoke to him in Gaia's voice.'

'Who's Gaia?'

'Goddess of all the worlds.'

'Hearing voices happens to humans too. What did Gaia tell him to do?'

'To go and bring Ragnarok to the world. Chaos. Bring the world to its knees and then claim it for the Elven. After that he stopped looking after us and began to strike at the power stations.'

Without thinking, he was holding his fingertips apart and letting sparks flash between them.

'I came back one day and he was talking really fast, right in my face,' he said sadly. 'Telling me he knew how to get the iron camps open. He told me about the abduction. He convinced us that the Watchers would have to give in.'

'You believed him?'

'Who else have we got? There's only Fen.'

Nell touched his arm and a little spark of static cracked. 'There's you. You're saving the Elven here, not Fen. You're looking after all the others, and making sure the little kids are happy. Giving Bean rides on your scooter.'

'Have you heard that kid cry?' he said, trying to make a joke of it, even now. 'He could wake the dead. Of course I'm kind to him.'

'That's better than causing chaos like Fen.'

He stared at the storm. 'Fen thinks big. I think small.'

Nell wouldn't give up. 'My mum's a police officer. She goes round the schools and talks to kids before they've had a chance to do bad things. But my dad's in the CID. They wage war on the criminals, they get to do the car chases and raids, and breaking down doors, all the exciting stuff. Thing is, I think my mum's way works best.'

She stopped, hardly able to hear herself talk any more. Around them, the massive, mutated trees had begun to creak and groan alarmingly.

'The storm's coming. It's a big one,' said Evan. 'I can take you back. Just you.' He glanced at Gwen, his face as expressionless as a mask. 'What's done is done. I'm sorry.'

'No.' She grabbed his hands this time. 'Please help both of us escape.'

He pulled away. 'He would track both of you down, and bring you both back.'

'I know you care,' she pleaded. 'You came to the school, you stayed, you hung around with me, you needn't have done.'

'I know.'

'And you warned me.'

'I was trying to make it not so wrong.' He gave a laugh. 'First time ever that I'd talked to a human.' His hair whipped around his face. 'I saw you watching Gwen. At first I thought you were jealous of her, then I saw that you were making sure that she wasn't going too far, that she wasn't becoming someone who really hurts others, rather than bosses them around and plays with their minds.'

'Yes.'

'Same with Fen. Except I can't stop him, so I go and do the power cuts, that way no one gets hurt.' His eyes met hers. 'But I can't stop this. No one stops Fen.'

She banged her fist down on the handrail, startling both of them. 'I thought you were going to be a friend. I really did. I thought we were laughing at the same things. Two outsiders together.'

He stared at her. 'We were. Except I'm not human. And we're enemies. Big problem.'

'Says who? A stupid story from long ago, about a couple who split up and had a custody battle about who was to get the kid? Crikey, there's tons of those around. No one wins, least of all the baby.' Her fist banged down again.

'No. Tell your brother this is stupid. End of problem.'

'He says this is war, and wars have casualties. He's says it's for the greater good.'

'That's what the Watchers say. It's stupid!'

But he wouldn't look at her any more. 'I just wanted to see my little sister before she forgets me,' he said, in a flat voice.

'If I get out, I swear I will get the addresses of the camps. Then you can let them out yourself. I'm good. I take after Dad and Nan. I've got a detective's brain, I can find out. I'll be your inside informer.'

'Sorry. I can't.'

She'd lost, but she still couldn't give in. There was one last chance, and she had to try it. She staggered as if the wind had blown her, and clutched the rail.

'What's wrong?' he said.

She crouched down. 'I feel like I'm going to faint.'

He knelt beside her. 'It's the storm. It sucks the oxygen out of the air.'

She kept her head low in case he could tell, like Fen, when she was lying. 'I need a glass of water.'

He looked at a cool box in the corner. 'Fen's got cans up here. Water's down on the ground.'

'I can't drink fizzy pop, I'm allergic. Water,' she said weakly.

He nodded. When he'd disappeared down the stairs, she sat up. She pulled the moon watch out of her pocket. The little ticking sun was so low, so near the cloud!

She had to wake Gwen right now.

Seventeen

'*Gsak, ma'forshlan orl kana.*'

Nothing happened.

'*Gsak ma'forshlan orl kana,*' she whispered again.

She watched Gwen's face. Nothing. She glanced around. Evan hadn't come back yet. She still had time.

She tried again. She could do this. She had an ear for words. Some people had an ear for music and could play a tune perfectly after hearing it once. She could recite a whole poem after one reading. She'd cursed her memory in the past because it made her remember whole arguments between her and her so-called friends, so that she replayed them over and over in her head at night when she couldn't sleep.

Now when she needed it she couldn't get it right.

She tried again, whispering the Elven words of waking. Nothing happened. She sat back on her heels. The words were right she was sure, so maybe it was like Chinese. In China you could say the same word in a high or a low voice and it would have different meanings – they sang their language. Everything about the Elven was musical. Evan had sounded as though he was half singing when he'd brought her out of the hex.

She tried again. She sang the words this time.

Gwen stirred. Quickly she sang them again. Gwen sat up, and rubbed her eyes. She looked like a sleepy princess in a very edgy mood.

'Did I fall asleep?' she groaned. Then she clutched her head. 'What did I drink? My head's hammering!'

Nell grabbed her hand and dragged her to her feet. 'It'll go away soon. But we have to run – now!'

Gwen had begun to look bewildered as well as bad-tempered. 'Who turned the music off? And where's Jake?' She looked around, wide-eyed. 'Where's my party?' she demanded.

'The warden came, we had to hide,' said Nell, desperately playing along. She tried to pull her to the central stairs, but Gwen wouldn't budge. For someone who spent her life nibbling on tiny little meals so that she could fit into her skin-tight outfits, she was a dead weight when she wanted to be.

'Oh, of course. I remember, I think,' she mumbled. She

wrapped her arms round Nell's neck, nearly smothering her. 'Aw babe, you're trying to save me from the warden! You wait, any time you want your hair straightened . . .'

A post-hexed Gwen was more trouble than a drunk Gwen, Nell decided, as she tried to steer her across the decking in the right direction.

'Yes, thanks,' she said quickly. 'But the thing is I saw Jake go off with Becca. We'd better go and find them.'

Gwen stopped, all ruffled feathers. 'Becca? I knew it! What a bitch.' She looked around. 'Where did they go?'

Nell sighed with relief and pulled her to the stairs. 'They're down here. Better hurry. He was kissing her.'

But Gwen's legs seemed to have turned to rubber.

'Here, put your arm round me,' said Nell, putting her own arm round Gwen's waist. 'You're trashed.'

Together they half fell, half walked down the winding steps.

Gwen raised a weak arm. 'Yay, party time!' she mumbled.

'Shhh. Don't let the warden hear, or he'll tell Mum. She'll go ape.'

Nell glanced fearfully at every balcony they came to, but so far no one took any notice of them. One more flight and they would be on the ground again. Suddenly Gwen's knees gave way and she fell forward. Nell caught her and staggered under the weight.

'Gwen! Gwen!' she hissed. But when that didn't work she slapped her sister in the face.

Gwen blinked. 'Did I fall asleep?' she said vaguely.

'Yeah, and now we've got to run and find Jake, before Becca hooks up with him.'

They slithered the rest of the way to the bottom and then, holding hands, they ran down the labyrinth of dark corridors.

'What is this place?' gasped Gwen.

Nell didn't get a chance to answer her. Two boys were suddenly in her path – the same two who claimed Fen was teaching them to be warriors. They were blocking the way to the oblong of light that was the doorway and freedom. They were both still in camo gear, like Falcon, and one was holding a bow, but he wasn't hunting rabbits this time. He was pointing it at them.

'What's happening?' he said.

The other one glared at Gwen. 'Did Fen wake the human?'

'My sister, you mean?' said Nell, feeling anger start to rise. She wasn't going to be stopped by two ten-year-olds, not now. 'Yes, he did, so move.'

The boys stayed where they were. Their faces became pointed, their eyes glittering and unreadable. 'We'd better ask him,' said the one with the bow.

'I'll go. You keep them here,' said the other.

Desperately, Nell reached into her pocket. 'Want some bubbly?' She held out the packet. The boy who'd walked off came back.

'No, go to Fen,' said his friend, still with bow aimed at them. 'I've got them covered.'

'No, you go.'

But it turned out that neither of them were going anywhere. There was a rush of air, and a figure in white appeared between them, like an apparition. It was Star. One moment she wasn't there, the next she was, calmly sucking the end of one of her tiny plaits.

Nell's heart sank. What now? She was hardly Star's favourite person. The Elven girl was staring at her and Gwen as though making up her mind about something. Then she turned to the two boys.

'Rex, Bran, go away.'

Nell held her breath. One boy began to growl, the other snarled, showing their teeth. 'No. You can't tell us what to do, Star. Something's going on with the humans.'

'I'm going to tell Fen,' said the other.

He moved but he didn't get far. Star pounced. She did a flying leap, with no effort, just like a cat, and somehow ended up behind the two boys, grabbing them by the scruff of their necks. Then her nose wrinkled, and suddenly she didn't look like a sweet, hippy girl. Her eyes narrowed, her face went sharp, her lips drew back and she became a spitting wild cat. 'You're not going anywhere,' she hissed.

'Give them the gum,' she said to Nell.

Nell obeyed. The two boys took it and then Star pushed them towards the hall where she could hear the rest of the Elven playing and talking, and where the smell of roasting meat was coming from.

When they didn't move, she stamped her foot.

'Go!' she ordered.

The two boys backed away with their prize. She watched them go and then shouted, 'Hey, Rex and Bran have bubbly. And they're not sharing!'

There was an immediate babble of little voices from the hall.

When Star turned round she was Little Miss Perfect again, although her eyes still glittered and her smile was slightly wicked, like a cat's. She brushed a plait across her cheek thoughtfully.

'I know what you're doing,' she said. 'And I think you're right. Fen's ill. One day I'll cure him. I know how, but I can't get near him.' She looked at Nell. 'Maybe I misjudged some humans.' There was a noise in the corridor behind them. A little Elven was coming towards them, moaning that she hadn't got any bubbly. Star turned back to Nell, more urgently now.

'Run,' she said. 'Maybe you can make it, maybe you can't.'

'Thanks.'

Their eyes met.

'May Gaia go with you.' Then Star turned on her heel, gathered the little Elven up and dissolved into the shadows.

Nell half dragged, half carried Gwen, bashing into either wall and stumbling, as they made for the light. With every step she expected to hear Fen's roar, but it didn't happen.

She pulled Gwen through the door and they were in the open air. She almost fainted with relief, but they had a long way to go yet. First they had to get out of sight of the palace.

Suddenly a flock of birds on the lilac tree screeched and flew into the sky, wings whirring. She looked around, her heart pounding, to see what had scared them, but there was nothing. Only a shadow on the ground that was growing bigger and bigger. Something was falling from above! She dragged Gwen back into the shelter of the doorway.

Just in time. A moment later Fen thumped in front of them, the ground shaking with the force of his landing, his knees bent, his white hair flying, his chalk-white face laughing horribly. The sound of bees was deafening.

'Gotcha.'

Eighteen

The forest creaked and groaned all around them, leaves rustled ferociously. There was a smell of electricity in the air, the storm was closing fast. Sparks flew from Fen's fingertips and hair.

Nell's heart sank, and not because of Fen or the weather. The sun was nearly down. The shadows were long. There was so little daylight left.

'I told you. She's no longer yours. She's mine,' Fen said. His mouth went up at the corners, his teeth showed, but it wasn't a smile. It was the grimace of a madman who thinks he's smiling. 'She'll no more hear your voice, human girl. She'll no more see your world, you've lost her.' He licked his lips. 'Or take her through the mist and watch her become old!'

Already one of his hands was snaking round Gwen's neck. His other was covering her mouth, stopping the scream that she was about to unleash. He looked terrible, his corpse-white face twitching and one eye flickering. He shook his head a couple of times, as though in pain. Then he dragged her over to the doorpost, and hit his head hard against it three times.

Nell backed away. The lilac tree was only a few metres behind her. She could smell its scent. Fen followed her, looking even worse now. Gwen hung in his arms, his hand over her mouth.

'Did Evan wake you?' he growled.

She took two or three more steps back towards the tree. 'No. The hex didn't work. I'm immune.'

'Liar. It was Evan.'

'You hit your own brother!' she said. She had to keep him talking.

Fen's eye started twitching again. He hoisted Gwen higher in his arms and came closer. 'He was trying to tell me what to do.' His lip curled. 'When he's my equal he can do that. Not before.'

She backed away. 'He's more of a leader than you are!'

His face contorted with fury. Even if she had a gun aimed at him, she wasn't sure it would it stop him. He looked invincible.

'Listen to me, human girl.' His eyes never left hers as he came closer and closer. 'Once upon a time, when we lived side by side, sometimes humans and Elven would be friends, sometimes they would fall in love. But that was then. Now Elven and human do not mix. Ever.' He thrust his face right at her. 'Evan is Elven. He's not your friend!' he roared. 'I won't allow him to be a traitor. Got it?' Drops of spit splattered her. 'So my advice is – run and save yourself.' His face twisted into the nearest thing she'd ever seen to a wolf's snarl. 'But your lovely sister is staying.'

He pushed Nell viciously in the chest, sparks snapping from his fingertips.

'Run, run while you can,' he sneered. 'I don't care about you. You're a grub, a caterpillar compared to Gwen. Go and tell the Watchers. I wish I could see their faces.'

He pushed her again. 'Go!'

She took a few more steps back. Not yet, she told him, silently.

'Funny, isn't it, you say you hate humans, but you spent a lot of time in our world,' she said.

He stalked after her, dragging Gwen along, her eyes popping. Good, she wanted him close.

'Our world, human girl. Our world first,' he growled. 'You were monkeys, we were elemental, next down from the gods. We taught you the things that made you human. Then you bred like ants until even though you were less powerful than us there were too many of you. You forced us to become the hidden folk.'

'It's no one's world,' she shouted back. 'It's just a world. You might as well say it belongs to the dinosaurs, they were here first.'

Fen snarled like a maddened wolf. 'No ant is going to keep us from being in the world. You know why? Because in the end we'll get back our power and you'll become the second class citizens.'

'And you're the one to do that?' she said sarkily, buying a little more time.

'That's right. You could've shared with us. We were never a threat until the Watchers got heavy. Now I bet they're regretting that move. I'll show them.'

One more step back and a branch poked into Nell's back. Lilac dust fell on her shoulders and hair. She'd made it to the memory tree. Something glimmered in the corner of her eye, amongst the blossom. It was just what she wanted.

'At least Evan looks after everyone. He cares,' she said. Keep him talking. Keep him angry at her – that wasn't hard. She slid her hand up as though grabbing a branch to steady herself. Her hand closed on the little sparkle of light.

'I heard you, human girl,' he snarled. 'Talking to Evan

about being friends. It was his idea to do so much research at the school. Not mine. Once I knew where to find the pair of you, I knew I could take you whenever I wanted. I should've known Evan had got himself involved. You're right, he's got a bleeding heart. He cares.'

'I can see that you don't.'

Inside her fist was her grandmother's little iron necklace.

'I care about trashing your human world, and that's all!' he said. He looked down at Gwen in his arms. 'Your sister's lucky to be stopping here . . .'

'Actually, she's not,' said Nell.

His eyes swivelled back to her, but he was too late. Her hand moved.

Maybe a gun wouldn't stop him. But a tiny iron chain – what would that do to him?

Quick as a cat she looped it over his hand. Against his white wrist it shone feebly. It was so fragile and insignificant, but not for Fen. He felt it burn straight away. It was worse than a bullet. His face changed. He let Gwen slide to the floor. He stared at his wrist in horror, and fell to his knees, holding out his hand as though acid was burning through the skin. Then he put his head back and howled like a wounded animal.

Nell watched him without pity. The chain weighed

hardly anything, but Fen's hand was sinking lower and lower as though it was being forced down by a ton weight. He was grounded, fixed to the earth. Her nan had refused to help, but her birthday gift had stopped Fen.

'Take it off!' His teeth were bared, half snarling, half in agony. 'Or you'll see what I'll do to you.'

'You'll do nothing,' said Nell, dragging Gwen out of the way. 'Evan told me. Iron weakens you, it takes away your power. You'll do nothing to me except swear and curse and stay on your knees.'

A scared face was watching from the doorway, chewing the end of a plait.

'Star,' Nell cried. 'I've chained him. I had to. Can you treat him now?'

'Yes,' the Elven girl breathed. 'Yes.' She walked out uncertainly, her eyes fixed on Fen. 'I have the fifteen crucial herbs, I can take the shadow away.'

They both looked down at Fen. He was still holding his hand, but his eyes had gone unfocused and dull.

'How long will it hold him?' said Nell.

'For as long as we want. Iron confuses us. He won't be able to take it off.' She turned in a whirl of plaits. 'I'll get my medicine box.' She ran to the door, then stopped and turned back. She bit her lip. 'Thank you.'

'You helped me too,' said Nell. She took Gwen's hand. 'Now we have to run.'

Gwen was staring at Star with a cross expression.

'Who's she?' she muttered. 'She wasn't invited to my party.'

'A gatecrasher. Ignore her.' Nell gave Star a wave, then tugged Gwen away.

Fen raised his head one last time. With a huge effort his eyes snapped into focus.

'You won't make it. You haven't got time,' he tried to shout, but his voice was slurred. 'The storm'll get you.'

He was right. Nell could feel it approaching on her skin, prickly and humid, the heavy air writhing around as though ghosts were breathing hot, stale air into their faces.

'And if it doesn't,' he mumbled spitefully, 'then the wolves will.' He whistled weakly through his teeth. 'Hey, Thor!' he tried to shout, but his eyes began to go dull again and his head was lolling forward.

Nell didn't wait to hear any more. She ran, dragging Gwen behind her. As they headed for the trees she heard Star shout, 'Evan! Quick, come here!'

She couldn't help it. She looked back. He was there in the great doorway, staring at her, a glass of water in his hands. Maybe that would be the last view she'd ever have of him.

Nineteen

Outrun the wolves. Outrun the storm.

The words hammered through Nell's mind.

A wind had picked up, blowing needles from the trees as though green rain was falling. Soon it would be real rain. She stared into the towering trees. Pathways branched off in all directions, each one dark, almost a tunnel. Any one of them could've been the path they took to get here.

'I don't know this part of the woods,' Gwen moaned. 'Are we lost?'

Nell peered into the growing darkness that was making everything look so menacing.

'Don't worry, I have the technology.'

She felt in her pocket and brought out the blue tracker torch she'd stolen from forensics. She switched it on and the bright, eye-watering beam cut through the darkness like a light sabre. She swept it back and forth across the rough ground – and there in front of her the little specks of blood she'd shed on the way here sprang out like crimson fairy lights.

Hansel and Gretel used crumbs to mark their path. This time the birds couldn't eat the trail and leave them stranded.

'Come on.'

There was no reply. She turned round. Her sister was staring at the trees, her face puzzled. 'Nell, where are we? Am I dreaming?'

Nell felt like screaming, but she knew Gwen couldn't help it. She'd been hexed and her mind was confused.

'Never mind,' she said, trying to be patient. 'It's going to rain. You don't want to get your hair wet, do you? That's why we have to run.'

Gwen nodded like an obedient child. They ran, Nell in the lead, sweeping the torch from side to side, following the bloody trail. Their steps were muffled by the carpet of needles underfoot, but they were assaulted on all sides by the rustle of small creatures, the howling of sudden breezes, and the creak and groan of the trees. When the path became overgrown they had to slow to a walk, Nell in the lead.

'Aw, it's beautiful,' breathed Gwen, from behind her.

Nell ignored her, scanning the ground with the torch for the next spot of blood. After a few more steps she realized Gwen wasn't following her.

She ran back.

'Hey, pretty little pony horse,' Gwen was cooing.

It was a foal, knock-kneed and adorable and pure white. It had eyelashes and huge eyes, and no horn yet, just a little bump on its forehead.

'So cute, the little horsey!'

Branches snapped as something big approached.

'But mummy horse isn't,' groaned Nell. 'Run now!'

Gwen stayed still. The mother unicorn was watching them from between the trees. Its horn was lowered like a lance, its white coat glowing in the semi-darkness. It was probably the same unicorn Nell had seen before. Maybe this was why it had attacked last time. Mothers with their babies were ferocious. Jackie certainly was. If she thought anyone had been picking on her girls then she'd march down to the school like a tiger.

'Don't touch it! Back away,' Nell warned, but Gwen tiptoed closer.

'I must be dreaming. So I can touch it.'

The unicorn lowered its head a little more. Its hoof came crashing down and scraped a huge gash in the undergrowth. Gwen didn't notice. She reached out a hand to pat the foal. The unicorn went berserk and reared up, its front legs windmilling. Nell rushed forward and tried to pull Gwen away, but she couldn't budge her. She was glued to the ground from shock. Her voice wasn't stuck, though. As the unicorn crashed back to earth, Gwen screamed hysterically in its face. It screamed back, showing its awful horse teeth.

Nell looked around for somewhere to hide. 'In here!'

The massive tree next to them had been struck by lightning at some point and the burned-out trunk was hollow. She pulled Gwen over to it. There was just enough space for the two of them to cram in.

'It's disgusting in here,' moaned Gwen, as the unicorn's horn hissed through the opening and tried to kebab them.

Nell pushed her further back. 'You want to be skewered?'

The spiralling horn lanced past them two more times, then the unicorn changed tactics. Its hoof thumped down and took a chunk of rotten wood out of the entrance. Nell took a peek.

'It's smashing its way in!'

Gwen was squashed into the farthest corner, her eyes glittering dangerously. She wasn't in a dream now. 'There are cobwebs in my hair,' she said ominously.

A massive thud shook the rotten tree. Gwen swore and held on to Nell as tightly as she used to when Nan told them scary stories.

'It's using its hind legs,' muttered Nell. 'It's trying to kick the tree down.' How could something so magical be so lethal?

There was another thud and then a tearing noise. A sliver of light shone on them. The creature's hooves had split the lightning-damaged trunk from top to bottom. A few more kicks and the unicorn would be inside with them.

Gwen closed her eyes angrily. 'This isn't my party. I want my party.'

'Yeah, well this time you don't get what you want. First time ever.'

Gwen pushed Nell away. 'Get off me. This is your fault.'

She moved only a few inches nearer the entrance but the unicorn sensed her. It thrust its nose in, nostrils flaring as it sucked in her scent, its breath steaming and stinking. Gwen swore and flattened herself against the rotten wood as its teeth snapped wildly together. Nell leaned forward and smacked it hard. It backed off. She turned to her sister, her own eyes glittering now.

'My fault?'

Gwen glared at her. 'I want my party. Not this freak show.'

Suddenly all Nell's fear turned to anger and boiled over. They should be running, but because of Gwen they were stuck in this stupid tree trunk with a raging unicorn outside. The whole thing was her sister's fault.

'Just shut up!' she hissed. 'Your party got us into this mess. You had to go and have it in the woods, didn't you? You never listen!'

'You would say that!' Gwen eyes went diamond-shaped and sparkled with tears. 'I know you hate me.'

They were eye to eye. 'Tough. I don't,' said Nell. 'Even though I might get trapped in this land with you for ever – which is worse than hell, believe me!'

The unicorn's hoof smashed into the wood again, showering them with splinters. They both moved back.

'Then you're stupid. You *should* hate me,' whispered Gwen. 'I treat you bad.'

'I tried to, but it doesn't work.'

Gwen pulled herself as far away as the trunk allowed. 'What does that mean?'

Nell glared at her sister. 'You're Gwen. You wouldn't notice if I did. You live in happy la-la Gwen land.'

A tear ran down her sister's cheek 'Who turned you into superbitchgirl?'

Nell could've screamed. 'You! Because we're stuck in a tree trunk and a unicorn is trying to kill us and all you do is feel sorry for yourself! No one else, just you.'

Gwen wiped her face, smearing it with dirt. 'What unicorn?' she said, in a small voice.

Nell stared at her. 'Huh?'

She sniffed. 'You might be Miss Cool, with your kookie outfits and your "I'm a loner" thing, but you don't know everything.'

'What don't I know?' said Nell, thinking, *Gwen thinks I'm cool?*

She wiped her nose on her sleeve. 'Like the fact that it's gone away?'

Nell listened. Gwen was right, there were no clouds of stinking breath, no splintering wood or snorting. They squeezed out of the trunk, brushing the cobwebs from their hair and clothes. The unicorn was metres away now, leading its foal into the trees, its tail swishing nervously. By the way it was tossing its head and looking around, something had spooked it.

'See,' said Gwen. 'I got something right.'

'You did,' said Nell, and because Gwen was like a puppy that needed praise, she smiled at her. Then she took the moon watch from her pocket and looked at it, and she didn't feel like smiling any more.

The first part of the sun was touching the cloud. And was that a tiny sliver of moon she could see appearing on the other side? She put it away.

One step at a time, she told herself. Stop worrying about how far we have to go, just put one foot in front of the other and keep Gwen moving. She scanned the gloom with the torch until she found the crimson spots of blood again. The spots led down a long straight path she remembered from her journey here.

'We could run,' she said. 'We used to like racing each other.'

Gwen gave a trembly smile. 'OK.'

So they ran as though they were young girls again and Jackie had taken them to the park. The torch beam flickered across the mosses and ferns that choked the ground, until it found each drop of bright, shining blood. It seemed easier now, even Gwen was keeping up. If it wasn't for the fleet-footed shadows that were keeping pace with them, Nell might have begun to feel hopeful.

No wonder the unicorn had run away. The wolves had found them.

On either side the grey shapes were moving through the dense forest as though they were a phantom escort. She tried to count them, but they flickered in and out of sight. Maybe ten, maybe more. Every now and then she caught the headlamp glow of their eyes. They were Thor's pack, but she couldn't see the old arctic.

As they ran she began to hear the sound of rushing water, and she realized they were near the place where she and Evan had met Falcon. This meant they had a long way to go, she thought with a sinking heart. She slowed to a walk and Gwen did the same.

Maybe it didn't matter any more.

The wind had died, leaving an ominous stillness. The storm was so close now. The air crackled with static. The trees opened out into the clearing, and the path led them straight to the little pool with the waterfall and the emerald green grass. The forest seemed to hold its breath. Even the animals had gone quiet.

'Thirsty. I want water,' said Gwen.

Nell put her arm out and stopped her.

Something was already there waiting for them. A white ghost, one that began making sinister little yipping noises when it saw them.

It was Thor.

'Why's that dog staring at us?' said Gwen.

Its pale blue eyes flickered from one to the other. A low growl issued from its throat. It was about to attack, but it never got the chance.

The leading edge of the storm hit the trees around them. Nell felt her hair start to stand out, like a dandelion clock, sticky with static. She looked at her sister. The same thing was happening to her.

With a flash of lightning that tore the sky and made a noise like a gigantic piece of silk being ripped apart, the storm broke over them.

Twenty

The thunder boomed and rolled. The heavens opened. Rain poured off the giant branches and cascaded down the trunks. It filled the pool and made the waterfall turn into a mini Niagara. It turned the ground into an instant bog. It deafened them both. It ran down their necks, it battered against their skulls, rushing, dripping, gurgling, and trying to drown them.

For a few moments Gwen gasped at her like a goldfish, the rain running down her face, her breath smoking in the suddenly frigid air. 'Stop!' she shouted above the flashes and rolls of thunder, as though even the weather should obey her.

It didn't. Nor did it make Thor back off. His eyes never left Nell. It was as though he hadn't even noticed the storm. The first time he'd seen her, she'd sprayed him with stinging perfume. He hadn't forgotten.

A low growl began to rattle from his throat. It wasn't loud but it had a certain quality that went straight through her ears into some part of her brain and pressed a button marked *ancient terror*.

Think, think, don't let fear take control, Nell told herself. Gwen was somewhere behind her, sobbing quietly to herself. The rain was hammering down so hard into the water it was creating a white mist that coiled clammily round their legs.

It was coiling around Thor as well.

The hair along his spine stood up like a brush. The smell of his wolf hunger was sharp in the air, his eyes merciless. He stalked closer, stiff-legged, his tail high, ready to fight this human that had dared hurt him. His jowls pulled back, his muzzle concertinaed into a ferocious snarl, his fangs glinting, the mist creeping round his legs. She held her hand out to him. He began to snarl, scraping a paw menacingly along the ground.

Nell felt a shiver go through her. Wolves weren't humans, they were animals, and animals only fought when necessary. If she could show Thor she was the stronger, he would give in.

The wolf stared at her. She stared back. If she looked away it would leap for her throat.

Say something! she told herself. She pointed her hand

towards the old wolf. 'Down!' she snarled. 'Bad dog!'

But it was no good. She was so tired and so wet. Evan had stopped Rikstall's dog so easily, but she wasn't good with animals. Even Faolan hated her.

The thunder rolled again, spooking Thor. He lowered his head, he gathered his feet under him. He prepared to leap at her.

'Down!' she screamed again, over the pounding rain. 'Don't you dare leap at me!'

The wolf stopped. Maybe she'd startled it. Maybe it was on the point of pouncing. She'd never know – because something else was coming out of the mist behind it. It was Gwen, moving strangely and twirling round in circles. She'd found a huge branch torn from a tree by the storm and she was whirling through the air as she spun on one heel, like a hammer thrower in the Olympics, getting maximum momentum. Nell hardly dared breathe. Time slowed. Nothing moved in the universe but Gwen. At the last moment Thor seemed to sense the movement and began to turn, but he was too late.

'Don't you bloody well growl at my sister!' shouted Gwen.

The branch hit the wolf right on the point of his jaw. Thor yelped and then went down as though felled by an axe.

'You leave her alone!' she howled as she spun on, unable to stop, for another couple of turns. 'Bloody gangster dogs.' Then she fell to her knees.

Nell ran over to her, leaping over the unconscious body of Thor. He was snoring like an old man.

'Thank you, Gwen,' she said in a small voice, and threw her arms around her sister. 'You cared.'

'Course I care!' She got to her feet, skidding in the mud. 'Like all those times I pretended to throw a tantrum because you were freaking out about Dad taking us on a day trip! And that psycho boy who used to chase you in the playground – I fixed him, didn't I?'

Nell blinked back tears. 'You never said.'

'Didn't have to. I'm your sister.' She looked around the clearing, wiping the rain from her eyes. 'You know what? I'm fed up with this party.' She threw the branch down. 'You're right. It's over. Come on, Nell, let's go home.'

Nell shook her head, raindrops spraying from her hair. 'Sorry. We can't. The rain has washed away the trail.' She wiped a mixture of rain and tears of frustration from her face. 'We're lost.'

Gwen's mouth dropped open. 'But we have to go home,' she said. Her lip quivered. 'I don't like this place. Do something.'

Nell let her own tears fall freely for the first time. 'I

can't. You've been here a day and a night and it's too late. We're here for ever.'

But Gwen wasn't listening. She was frowning at something over Nell's shoulder.

'More dogs.'

Nell spun round. The rest of the pack were approaching from the trees in a semicircle. Ten lean, slinking wolves; brindle, grey, black, steaming in the rain. They began to make the sinister yapping sounds again. Their leader was down and they weren't sure what to do. The big brindle wolf stepped forward and sniffed at Thor's unconscious body. It tipped its head back and gave a howl. That really disturbed the others. They began milling about, yowling and snarling. The brindle's yellow eyes fixed themselves on Nell. It stepped over Thor and came closer.

Nell bent down and picked up Gwen's branch. 'Stay behind me,' she said, but she knew it was hopeless. They couldn't fight off a pack of wolves.

Something howled from inside the trees and the wolves turned to look.

'More of them!' moaned Gwen.

'So?' said Nell. 'It doesn't matter whether it's ten or twenty, we're not going to win.'

The brindle seemed to agree. It was edging closer to

her. But the other wolves were acting oddly now. Their tails were going down and they were turning towards the trees. Something was approaching and it wasn't a friend of theirs by the look of their tails.

A moment later Faolan catapulted out of the trees. Nell gave a groan. One more hostile wolf. The high-pitched snarl echoing from her curled muzzle was vibrating her whole body. This was what had disturbed the wolves. They began backing away, but Faolan ignored them. She had one goal and that was Nell.

'Why?' whispered Nell. 'I never hated you.'

Faolan stalked closer, the threatening growl rumbling all the time. Nell held her breath. Was this the end? The wolf hopped right up to her. She gave Nell another of her supercilious glares and then, like a well-trained dog, came and stood to heel, at her side. Nell nearly fainted.

The horseshoe of wolves stared. Faolan's growl rose in pitch. It was a warning. Touch her and I'll get you.

The wolves began to back away, all except the brindle. It began growling back at Faolan and taking small steps forward.

If they fought, it would win. Faolan was much smaller and lame. But it didn't matter because someone else was coming out of the trees. It was Evan, making little growls and snarls, fixing his gaze on the brindle, staring it down.

The wolf didn't like that. It rose up, its legs stiff, its back fur bristling. It lowered its head, but Evan didn't flinch. He circled it, yowling, whispering to it in wolf. Everything about him, his movements, the curl of his lip, the sound of his voice, was wolf not boy.

The brindle stood it for as long as he could then he took off after the others.

'Do I know him?' mused Gwen, as Evan gave one last growl and chased the brindle from the clearing. When he came back Nell could see that he was still in wolf mode, although he was shrugging every now and then as though he was trying to get back to being a boy.

Gwen frowned. 'Oh, it's that kid from school. The one you fancied. Why am I dreaming about your mystery boy?'

Nell ignored her. Over the drumming of the rain came another noise – a noise from her world, echoing into this Elven land. It was the sound of the church bells, and they were chiming the hour. *One . . . two . . . three . . . four.* They were ringing for five o'clock. The time of sunset.

As the last bell began to echo across the forest, Evan came up to them, his hair flattened by the rain, water dripping down his face.

'You saved us, but it's too late!' she cried.

She couldn't believe it. He gave his twisty grin.

'No, it isn't.' He put an arm round her waist, and one round Gwen's. 'Hang on.'

Caution for New Mothers

Be warned about the Elf-King's daughter. Remember how she was left here by her father? It is she who tainted mankind's blood with that of the Elf. It shows itself now and then in unfortunate babes.

So guard well, mothers, check your children for excessive trickery, for the power of hex and curse. Test them mightily with iron. Are they as beautiful as starlight, as fierce as wolves, as cold as ice? Yes? Then you have a changeling, a relic of the Elf-King. Purge it with bitter herbs. And do not spare the rod, beat the Elf blood from it with vigour.

Eighteenth-century warning for new mothers
Granny Ballard's Herbal Midwifery, 1795

Twenty-one

Speed, incredible speed. The world became a blur. Until that sudden, jarring brake that tore at every cell in Nell's body and made her brain feel as though it was ricocheting off the inside of her skull.

Her feet touched the ground and she stumbled forward a few paces, tripped and ended up on her knees. The white stepping stones were beneath her. She was in the mist, deep inside where it felt as though the air was made of jellyfish.

They were home. She could smell her world, with its tang of exhaust fumes. The pounding rain had stopped. She heard Gwen groan, and she followed the noise of retching, the mist thinning around her. Gwen was on her knees, Evan crouched beside her.

'Is she OK?' said Nell.

'Do you mean is she a hundred years old? No. We made

it with a few seconds to spare. She's only got one little souvenir.'

'It's not a wrinkle is it? She'll go mad.'

At that moment Gwen sat up and then got to her feet. 'I am never drinking cider ever again,' she declared.

Nell stared at her. Gwen now had a white streak down one side of her hair. Because it was Gwen it looked amazing, but Nell decided to let her find out about it later. There were other more important things to find out. She turned to Evan.

'Why did you change your mind and help us?'

He shrugged. 'I'm not Fen. I'll save the Elven in my own way.'

She touched a finger to the bruise on the side of his cheek. 'He hit you. What'll happen when you go back?'

'Last thing I saw was Star doctoring him.' He pulled a pretend scared face. 'When Star doctors someone, they stay doctored until she stops.'

He put his arm around Gwen and began hopping over the stones. With every step the mist got thinner. At last he stopped.

He looked everywhere but at her. 'I've got to go,' he said. 'You're safe now.'

The world paused for Nell.

'So you forgive me? For lying to you.'

He glanced at her from under his hair. 'It was the only thing you could do.' He gave a weak smile. 'I would've done the same.'

'Will I see you again?' she said, as casually as Hélène would.

'Who knows?' He unwrapped his arm from around Gwen and leaned her against Nell. 'You've got Gwen, but we won't get our parents back. It's only a matter of time before they catch me or the rest of the Rivers.'

She stared at the ground, kicking her toe on the white stone. 'I told you. I'll get the addresses of the camps.'

'You won't. You can't, not even you.'

She looked up. 'Sundown tomorrow. Please. Meet me.'

He shook his head. 'It won't change anything. We'll have to remember to be born the same species next time.'

She just stood there, holding on to Gwen. She knew she should be feeling happy that she was back safe and sound, but she wasn't. There seemed to be a large stone in her chest that was stopping her breathing. 'I wish the world was different.'

Evan looked away. 'So do I. But it isn't. This is goodbye.'

'Give me a night and day. I'll get you those addresses.'

He gave another sad smile, totally unconvinced, the

mist folding around him like chiffon. 'Yeah, course you will, human girl.'

'I will. You'll see.

But the mist had taken him. She stared into its slowly churning depths, and blinked back tears. He didn't realize, no one realized, just how determined she could be.

Gwen was staring fretfully at her mud-covered hands and nails.

'Oh my God, where am I?' she said in horror. She looked down at the state of her clothes and shoes. 'I'm filthy. I smell! What's happening to me?'

Nell linked arms with her. 'I rescued you,' she said. 'You got lost in the woods. You must have hit your head. You've been babbling all sorts of rubbish.'

Gwen's eyes were round with horror. She began to shake and then tears began to pour down her cheeks.

'Gwen?' called a wavering voice from close by. It was the sort of voice that had been hoping and praying and has now heard something but can't quite bring itself to believe. 'Is that you crying, Gwen? Please say it is!'

Nell gave a laugh and pulled her along. They ran out of the mist into a damp October teatime.

'Mum?' wailed Gwen.

They were both there, Jackie and Church, standing on

the path that led down to the mist as though they'd been there all day. Jackie gave a scream and ran towards them.

'Gwen! How? Where?' she stammered, losing all her police officer cool. She gathered Gwen into her arms. 'And Nell!'

Church just stared. First at Gwen, then his eyes swivelled and fixed themselves on Nell.

'Hello, Dad,' she said, as innocently as she could, over the sobbing and squeals of Gwen and Jackie. 'She got lost. She wasn't taken. No kidnappers. We're both OK.'

His hand came up to his ear. 'Johnny?' he said into his mobile. 'We've found them. Call it off. We're in the hollow. Give us a few minutes.' He dropped his hand. His eyes never left Nell.

'The miraculous reappearance of my daughters from the mist,' he said slowly. He seemed to be trying to read her thoughts through her eyeballs.

'Yes,' she managed.

'Mi-ra-cu-lous,' he repeated, stretching every syllable and imbuing each one with a hint of sarcasm.

'Erm. How come you were waiting here?' said Nell, just as slowly.

'Oh, we've been waiting here all day!' he said grimly. 'It's a popular spot. Your grandmother's been haunting the place – coming down here on the hour, with a face like thunder. Shouting into her phone. Saying she's going to break some rules. Saying that she's quitting.' He raised an eyebrow. 'You were with her before you ran off. Any of that make sense to you?'

Nell stared back. 'She's old, maybe she's losing the plot?'

'So you wouldn't know about the man with her. The one who says he's an expert on tracking people in woods, but who looks like MI5?'

'No.' Nell looked around. 'Where is she?'

Church didn't get a chance to answer. Jackie staggered over, beaming and crying at the same time, her arms still round Gwen.

'Never do that to me again, Nell,' she said softly. 'When Dru said you'd run away, I nearly went crazy!' Her face was puzzled and relieved at the same time. 'And you cut your hair! This is so bizarre.' She tilted her head to one side. 'But I like it.'

'Too late if you didn't.'

'Cheeky.'

A little howl came from Gwen. 'Mum, please, I'm the victim,' she said impatiently. 'I'm traumatized. I need all your attention for ever and ever.'

Jackie laughed and hugged Gwen again. 'Where did you find her?'

Nell could feel her father's eyes boring into her.

'Tunnels,' she said, desperately making it up as she went along.

'Your mother made us search the mist ten times,' said Church. 'Your grandmother's been walking up and down for hours. None of us noticed any tunnels.'

'Only a few kids know about them,' she lied. 'They're hidden World War Two tunnels. Under the brambles.'

'Really?' His eyes were like laser beams. 'Not pirate tunnels, or secret alien bases?'

She kept her cool. 'That would be silly.'

'Show me,' he said.

Seconds turned into what seemed like hours as her brain tried to come up with something. 'They collapsed as we came out,' she said, eventually. 'Completely waterlogged.'

'So that's why you're both soaking wet,' exclaimed Jackie. She kissed Gwen's forehead. 'Leave them alone for now, Church. Let's get them both checked out and in dry clothes before they freeze.'

As they walked out of the hollow, they could hear the shouts going up around the woods. Officers were letting each other know that the search was over. Church gave her one last glowering look.

'Don't move an inch,' he said, and went over to update them.

This left Nell staring at her grandmother.

In the growing darkness Druscilla Church was standing by the broken iron railings, in her leathers. When she saw Nell a look of immense relief washed over her face. For the first time ever, she looked close to tears.

The man standing next to her didn't look tearful, though. He wore a black suit that looked out of place in the wild wood. His shiny shoes were covered in mud. No way was he an expert on tracking. Behind Dru, on either side, were two men Nell had never seen before. I must take after my dad, she thought, even I can tell that they're guards of some kind.

She walked over, but not too close.

'You were right, Nan. Fen let her go.'

Dru's eyes sparkled sadly. 'No, he didn't, Nell love. You rescued her. He would've kept her there.'

Nell moved nearer, and lowered her voice. 'You betrayed the Rivers, Nan,' she said bitterly. 'You told me that you tried to do the best for them. But Evan says they asked for a truce – and then you captured them.'

Dru winced. 'I didn't know. I swear.' She shot a glance sideways. The man gave her a warning look, but she ignored him. 'Those above me planned it,' she said defiantly.

The man must have given the guards a signal because

they closed in on Dru. She shrugged them away.

'You did the right thing, Nell,' she said loudly. 'You went in there and saved her. I was kidding myself, thinking that Fen would have given her up.'

'He's ill. He won't be a trouble again.' Nell turned to the man. 'And nor will Evan, so leave them alone. It's over.'

He had the coldest eyes she'd ever seen. 'It will never be over,' he said. 'You have valuable information. We'll have to debrief you.'

She remembered Evan saying that they'd be killed if anyone knew the Harps were failing. 'Don't bother. I don't remember anything.'

'You have no choice,' he said.

She backed away.

'Do you know why we're immune?' she said, looking round at them.

Dru glanced at the man. 'We don't know for sure. Something genetic.'

'Fen says that in the past Elven and human used to fall in love. Did they have babies, like the Elf-King and his girl?'

'In the past, maybe,' said the man. His lip curled in distaste. He was as bad as Fen.

Nell nodded. 'Then I think we're immune because we have a drop of Elven blood in our veins.' She pointed at him. 'All of us. Including you.'

She turned on her heel to walk away but one of the guards was now at her side.

'Sorry, Nell,' the man called coldly. 'In the interests of national security, you have to come with us.'

'So you can give me the treatment? No, I don't want to forget.'

'First you talk, and then we take all your worries away,' he said. He nodded to the guard, who grasped her arm.

Nell kicked out at him. 'I don't want it!' she shouted.

Dru rushed forward. 'Nell, quiet! It's no use.'

Nell kicked the guard again, but he wouldn't let go. 'Dad! Dad!' she screamed.

'What's up?' Church came trotting out of the darkness towards her. 'What's going on?'

She peeled the guard's hand from her and ran towards him. She held up the tracker torch.

'Arrest me. I stole this from forensics.'

He frowned at her. 'Don't be daft. I'm not arresting you for that.' He gave the man in black a fierce look, then glanced over at Dru. 'Mum? What's going on here?'

Nell pulled his arm fiercely. 'They won't tell you. Please. Take me away.' She stared at him, let him see the desperation. He didn't understand, but he caught on.

'Oh, the tracker torch! I heard one had gone missing.

Nell, I'm disappointed in you. This is pretty serious.' He lowered his voice. 'Do you want cuffs?'

'No!'

He put a heavy hand on her shoulder. 'You'd better come with me. We'll get this sorted at the station.' He glanced back at his mother and the others. 'Catch you later, Ma.'

As they walked to his car, there were a few reporters milling about, but one of Church's glares soon made them back off.

'Well, Twigs, I've no idea what that was all about,' he said, as they got in. 'But how about a burger?'

'Yes. And I need to talk to you.'

He turned the key. 'No problem.'

She did up her seat belt. 'But this time you have to listen.'

He put his arm along the seat and backed the car out of the alley. 'We've talked before.'

Nell pretended to think. 'Oh, right, yes. I remember. Those few seconds of your time were so precious, how could I forget?'

Their eyes met in the rearview mirror. 'When did you get sarcastic?'

She smiled. 'Always have been. You never listened.'

Twenty-two

The police station was too hot and the air was like dust. Nell always thought this, but it was even more so after the Elven forest. She'd been home and got clean clothes, but she could still feel that fresh, icy air on her skin and smell the tang of pine.

The building stood at the top of a hill, so she was leaning on a windowsill and looking out at the dark town with its strings and swirls of orange streetlights and blocks of lighted windows.

On the other side of town the hospital rose, its windows alight too. Gwen was in there, being mollycoddled and fêted. The news crews had interviewed everyone, and then packed up and gone. Half the reporters thought it was some teenage prank, the other half suspected that she'd run off with a boy and then changed her mind.

Questions about teenage drinking were being

discussed on BBC news.

Gwen's gang had extended their shrine to include messages of happiness that their queen had returned home safely. They were probably queuing up in the hospital corridors waiting for an audience with her at this moment. Maybe they'd already got a white streak down the front of their hair to match Gwen's. If they hadn't it wouldn't be long before they did. Her Facebook page was buzzing.

The door to the office opened and Church came in, kicking it shut behind him. He handed her a thick brown paper bag. 'Burger, fries, the works. Tuck in.'

For once he'd got it right. Suddenly she felt ravenously hungry – like a wolf probably. She ripped the bag open and ate like she'd never stop.

When she'd nearly finished, she said without looking up, 'Stop staring. It's creepy.'

Her father leaned back in his chair. 'You've changed, Twigs.'

'New hair,' she said, through a mouthful of fries.

He shook his head slowly. 'More than that. You've come into focus.'

She licked her finger and sat back, full at last. 'I was always in focus. It was your eyes that were out of focus, when they looked at me.'

He waited until she'd screwed the paper bag up and wiped her hands. 'Come on, spill the beans. What really happened to you and Gwen?'

He tried to do the policeman's stare on her, tried to pin her down, but she wasn't afraid of him any more. She returned his gaze for a while, then said, 'I know why you hate the scent of pine.'

He frowned and rubbed his ear. 'I don't see what that has to do—'

'And I know why you always touch your ear when you're angry or upset.'

He dropped his hand.

'Now you're being creepy,' he said.

She smiled. 'OK, Dad. You really want to know the truth?'

He went to reach for his ear again, but stopped himself. 'Yes.'

'Well, I'll tell you. You won't believe me at first, you never do. You won't listen, you never do. But I'll tell you. And it all begins with your mother, my Nan, Druscilla Church.'

And so she told him. All about the Elven and the Watchers and the secret war that was being waged between the two. She told him about the iron camps and the Elven land beyond the mist. She told him how she'd rescued

Gwen and how Evan, an Elven boy who should have been her enemy, helped save them both at the end.

And she told him about Druscilla Church, a Watcher because she had an ability to withstand the Elven charm, and that she, Nell, had inherited that gift – or curse.

When she'd finished Church, who'd heard the confessions of robbers, murderers, serial killers and psychos, sat with his mouth hanging open and a burger drooping forgotten in his hand.

'Told you that you wouldn't believe me,' she said.

'It's asking a bit much,' he said, but something wasn't right with his voice. He seemed to be having a struggle inside. The remains of the burger dropped from his fingers and he stood up and began to pace up and down.

'So the house I grew up in is made of iron to protect us from a race of fairyfolk . . .'

'Yes, Dad. Deep down you know it's true.'

'Me and your grandmother, we had a strange relationship. My childhood was odd. She wasn't there. I had babysitters. You won't believe it but I was a scared kid. Nightmares – oh God, the nightmares.'

He kicked a waste basket out of the way and carried on walking. 'I remember something from when I was very small,' he said, and stopped. 'I remember a face at the window and Mum telling me to go to my room. A white face. And the smell of pine!' He ran a hand over his own face. He was sweating heavily.

Nell took her mobile out of her pocket and flicked through the images until she came to the one of Evan. She held it out to her father. He backed away, going pale.

'It's a teenage boy, that's all,' he said desperately.

He really was taking this badly.

'So why are you now standing in the corner like a naughty schoolboy?' she said.

Church looked around. He was indeed pressed into the corner of the room. His hand went to his ear. 'Because suddenly I'm scared and confused and I'm never scared or confused any more.'

'It's the Elven, Dad. I think you're immune too, but Nan gave you a treatment thinking it would make you forget. Only it didn't altogether work.'

Church looked at her, horrified.

'White hair, Nell. And dark, dark eyes,' he whispered. She nodded. 'And they move like the wind, sometimes here, sometimes there, nothing in the middle, like they can teleport.' When she nodded again, he gave a sigh of relief. 'Oh, Lord. I thought I was getting abducted by aliens. Or going crazy. I didn't dare tell anyone in case they put me in a mental home.'

'Well, I suppose in a way they are aliens, aren't they?'

said Nell. She took her father's hand and led him back to the desk and made him sit down.

'What treatment did she do on me?' he said, in a dazed voice.

'It's an operation on the ear. The right ear,' she said. 'They put a little metal implant under the skin.'

Church stared at her, then put his hand up to his ear. 'Yes, I have that. But it's for my asthma. I used to wheeze as a child, Mum said—' He stopped. 'It's not for asthma, is it?'

Nell shook her head.

He stared at the wall for a while, breathing heavily. Nell could almost see his brain ticking over. 'That explains a few things,' he said. 'I told her about the face at the window. She could've told me the truth. But she took me to this place. She said it was Chinese acupuncture or something, to cure my asthma. I never saw the face again. But when I first joined the force I had a medical and the police doctor told me there was nothing wrong with my lungs at all. I'd never had asthma or anything like it.' He stood up, his chair sliding back and hitting the wall. He was breathing rapidly. 'I need to talk to her, now. And that man with her.'

'No. Not yet. Calm down,' she said. 'I think she did it because she didn't want her child or her grandchildren to have to do the things that she does.'

'Hmmm.' He stood up. 'Excuse me a moment.'

He went out. A while later she heard a shout of pain from one of the washrooms down the corridor. Then he came back in, holding a tissue to his ear. He threw something tiny down on to the desk. It was one of the tiny infinity implants.

She leaned forward. 'That man wants to do the treatment on me, Dad. But I don't want him to. I want to remember.'

He took her hand. 'Let them try, Twigs. I've never liked secret organizations – even if my own mother is running part of it! There's no one to police them. Someone's got to watch the Watchers so it might as well be me.' He was staring at her as though he'd never seen her before. 'More importantly, Twigs, for the first time in thirteen years you've opened up to me.'

'And you've actually stopped and listened to me. Instead of treating me like an expensive nuisance that you dislike.'

That stunned him. 'I don't dislike you.' He hesitated and then wiped a hand over his eyes. 'I suppose sometimes you brought back bad memories of all that happened between your mum and me. It's funny, everyone thinks Gwen is the rebellious one, but she's not. It's you.' He looked down at her. 'I could never control you. You ignored me, showed your dislike. You didn't even take my name.'

She stared back. 'Why should I?'

'I am your father,' he said, in a hurt voice.

'That's just a word. Fathering takes more than a visit now and again,' she said. 'You've got to earn dadhood.'

He gave her a worried look. 'Have we read each other wrong, Twigs?'

'Yes. But it can change. And my name's . . .' For a moment she was about to say Hélène, but she didn't need her any more. '. . . my name's Nell. Or maybe Ellena for posh.'

'Understood.' He held out his arms and enveloped her in a tentative hug that smelled of his aftershave and leather. 'And now,' he said, in her ear. 'What do you want in return?'

She pulled away. 'Who says I want anything?'

He raised an eyebrow. 'You're a Church, you might not use the name but you are. You pulled off the rescue of a kidnap victim that even a trained team of negotiators and officers couldn't have done. You've spilled the beans. It's for a reason.'

Here it was, the important bit. Her mind went back to the Red House kitchen, and Dru's strained face, trying to explain to her why Gwen could not be rescued, and trying to make her see that the iron camps were needed. *I've just come back from one*, she'd said.

'I promised Evan something, Dad. And I need your help to keep it,' she said. 'I want you to go and find Nan's passport without her or that man knowing, and find out where she travelled to last. Then I want you to help me find a certain place that will be nearby.'

'Let me guess. An iron camp.'

'Smart.'

'OK, Twigs – oops – Nell. It's a deal.'

They were in the living room when Jackie got back from the hospital. Nell was at the PC by the window. Church was lounging with his laptop.

'Tom,' said Jackie suspiciously. 'You've got your feet up on my sofa. What's going on? I thought you were going to visit Gwen. That's why I left her. You know how clingy she gets when she's off-colour.'

He waved a nonchalant hand. 'She's fine. The young doctors are keeping her amused.' He winked at Nell. 'I've got more important things to do.'

Jackie narrowed her eyes and looked from one to the other. 'What's going on?' she muttered.

Nell stopped scrolling for a moment. 'He's helping me

with something, Mum. You always wanted us to do things together.'

He pressed a few buttons. 'Try 57 north 150 east. What's that?'

'Been there already,' said Nell. 'It's some kind of army base. Nothing to do with us.'

'What are you looking at?' said Jackie, mystified.

Tom scrolled on patiently. 'Kamchatka.'

'Huh?'

'That's the last place Mum visited. Siberia. The most desolate isolated spot on the whole planet.' He clicked on something, examined it, and then went back to scrolling. 'It's the size of France, Belgium and Luxembourg all rolled into one, and hardly anyone lives there. It's amazing, it's all volcanoes, snowfields, forests and unimaginably lonely shores.'

Jackie plonked down on the other end of the sofa. 'Why on earth would Dru go there? It's hardly the sort of place to find fairytales.'

Nell and Church looked at each other, smiled secretly and then went back to Google Earth. He'd had to break into the Red House, he'd told her. Dru wasn't there and the place had been locked up. Luckily her passport was still in her desk drawer.

'This is going to take all night,' he said, with relish.

'Nothing beats me. Not even Kamchatka.'

In the end even Jackie got her laptop and joined in.

'What are we looking for?' she said, bringing up the program.

'Some kind of camp far away from anywhere. You should be able to zoom in and see high fences round it.' Nell looked up to find Jackie frowning at her. 'It's for a school project,' she said innocently.

Jackie looked at them both. 'Come off it. I know you two have got some sort of bizarre secret going on,' she said. 'I'm so pleased.'

'Pleased we have secrets? Why?' said Nell.

'Anything as long as you have something between you,' said Jackie.

After that the room fell silent as they scrolled over volcanoes, lakes, mountains and hidden valleys.

In the end it was Jackie who spotted it. A tiny speck in the midst of snow, ice, endless forests and not another living soul within a thousand miles.

They gathered round her laptop and stared at the little blip. Then Jackie zoomed in until it could be seen clearly – a settlement of huts surrounded by a huge, heavily constructed fence. A single road led to it. Mountains and huge forests cut it off from everywhere else.

'That's it,' breathed Nell.

Twenty-three

The stale air of the hospital was being gently perfumed with green apple chewing gum.

Half of Gwen's class were in the corridor, with cards and flowers. At the front of the queue were Becca and the rest of the gang. They had the biggest bunches and the biggest cards, collages they'd made by cutting out hundreds of photos of Gwen and gluing them on to a big background. Nell walked past them all.

'Hey, wait,' said Becca. 'We're her friends. We go in first.'

Nell ignored her.

'It's Gwen's rules,' Becca insisted. 'She said that we could be the first to go in, and also anyone that is currently allowed to sit on our lunch table. Which isn't you.'

Nell stared at her. 'You know your special table? Well

I'm going to make sure I get there first from now on, and I'm going to invite all the uncool kids to sit with me. Then you'll have to find another.'

'What's up with her?' she heard Bria mutter to Paige. They'd tagged on the end of the queue, as usual.

She turned on them. 'Don't you remember how we used to laugh at Gwen and this lot, with their rules? Instead we used to spend our time making our own programmes with our camcorders. It was such a laugh. But now you do nothing except follow Gwen around, or text your boyfriends. It's like part of your brains have gone to sleep. Why don't you just think for yourself again, for once?'

They all stared at her. No one said anything, so she stalked by, and immediately they got in a huddle and she heard the word *freak* whispered, although loud enough so she would hear.

It didn't bother her one bit.

'Hey, sis,' Gwen said weakly, as Nell came into the room.

She was looking pale, but beautiful, with a stylish bandage round her throat. The white streak in her hair looked pretty cool as well.

'The doctor says it can happen when people get a fright,' explained Gwen. 'Or maybe I got hit on the head, that's why I can't remember anything. The doctor says I'm lucky, my hair might have turned completely white.' She paused and frowned. 'Which is maybe why I keep dreaming about this funky man with white hair. Weird.' She was looking at herself in the shiny side of one of the medical machines surrounding her. 'Suits me, I think,' she said weakly.

The bedside table was covered in cards, flowers and presents, but Nell managed to squeeze her little bunch of lilac blossom into one of the vases. Gwen looked startled when she saw them, and leaned forward to smell their heavy scent.

'What does this remind me of?' she said in a small, tight voice.

'The tree at home?' said Nell. It was funny that both her and Evan's homes had lilac trees outside. Now every time she went into the garden she could think of him.

'No, something else,' said Gwen. Her face had begun to look tragic. 'I keep sort of remembering some really odd stuff. Me and you in a forest. And wolves. Nan's been to visit. She says it's all alle-gori-cal.'

Nell said nothing. After a moment Gwen screwed her face up. 'What does that even mean?'

'Means you've been dreaming about another world, where fairy folk live.'

'Dreaming?'

'Yes,' said Nell, firmly. 'You're safe and sound now. You can carry on enjoying your life in that special Gwen way, just like you always have.'

Gwen's lip began to tremble, and a tear rolled down her cheek.

'Hey, what's wrong?' said Nell. This wasn't like her sister at all. She was getting huge amounts of attention; there was a crowd of friends outside waiting to see her. That would usually keep her happy for days.

'None of you get it,' Gwen cried. 'I've been lying here and suddenly I realized that in a few months I'll be leaving Woodbridge, and I'm scared.' She sniffed and wiped the tears from her face. 'All through school I've had everyone in my power! But when I leave it'll change. I want my life to be like this for ever – with Jake and my mates and the parties in the woods.'

'The next step will be as good,' said Nell.

'No it won't.' Gwen gave her a sad look. 'Your glory days are to come,' she said. 'But these are mine. I'll never pass my exams, I'll never go to college.'

'Shame,' said Nell. 'Marrying a footballer takes quite a few skills. You'll need maths so that you can add up your credit cards for one thing.'

Gwen picked at the bed-sheet fretfully, but she gave

a weak smile. 'And languages in case my husband gets transferred.'

'And geography so you know where you're going when they play abroad.'

'PE to keep my figure,' added Gwen. 'And then I'll get loads of freebie clothes and make-up.'

'And if it doesn't work out, you'll always have a pocketful of dreams,' said Nell, in a soppy voice.

Gwen gave a giggle, but it didn't last. Her mouth turned down again. 'Are Mum and Dad still fighting about me having the party in the woods?'

'No. They were sitting chatting when I left.'

'It won't last,' said Gwen. 'I used to hate hearing them argue. I couldn't stop it. Do you think that's why I control everyone else?'

Nell perched on the edge of the bed. 'Yeah. I did the opposite. I opted out. Went for a dreamworld.'

'We should meet in the middle,' said Gwen. 'Then perhaps we'd be two normal sisters.'

They stared at each other.

'Nah,' said Nell. 'That'd be boring.'

They began sniggering, and then laughing. It was slightly hysterical laughter, and Gwen had to keep wiping her eyes, but it did them both good.

'We're the Church sisters, babe,' said Gwen, when she

could breathe. 'We're supposed to be dysfunctional.'

She wiped her eyes for the last time and looked at Nell thoughtfully, as if seeing her for the first time.

'OK, you've hacked your hair off with nail scissors and somehow managed to end up with this ragamuffin cut that suits you, but something else has changed.' Her eyes widened. 'You found a boy?'

'No.'

Gwen shook her head slowly. 'Seriously. There's a look when a girl meets someone significant.'

'The only boy I met is my imaginary one,' Nell answered cautiously.

Gwen rolled her eyes. 'For a minute there, I thought my little sister had grown up. Daydreamer. Start living for real, like me.'

'I'll try,' said Nell, gathering her things together.

Luckily for her, Gwen's butterfly attention was diverted by Becca poking her head round the door.

'I'm going anyway,' said Nell. She slung her schoolbag over her shoulder and picked up her clipboard.

'Why are you carrying those?' said Gwen.

'It's just some homework,' said Nell vaguely.

Gwen groaned and gave her an exasperated look. 'Your beloved sister was lost in the woods and you're doing *homework*! You really are a geek, Nell. You never change.'

'No, I don't,' she agreed. 'I'm the same me I've always been. Only I didn't realize it.'

Twenty-four

The lifts weren't working in either Rowan House or Beech House.

Nell's leg muscles twanged but she walked wearily up another flight of steps. Then she counted the doors along and checked her chart, to make sure she'd got the right one. She knocked.

'Hello,' she said, when a woman answered. She gave her sweetest Gwen-like smile. 'I'm from Woodbridge Community College, and I'm doing a project on energy saving and I wonder if you would take part in a small experiment . . .'

It was funny what people would agree to do if you told them it was for a school project.

After an hour of knocking, Nell stood on the roof of Rowan House. Woodbridge Road, the church and the woods were spread out before her. Which meant that anyone coming out through the mist would see these tower blocks.

She checked the time, then she walked all the way back to the church beside the alley. She sat on the wall. Gradually the world grew dark around her and night fell. The streetlights came on, the shops and the houses switched their lights on, everyone thankful that there had been no more power cuts.

The tower blocks across the road were two tall rectangles of light that reached into the night sky.

She checked the time again. Thirty seconds to blast-off. She counted it down.

'. . . three, two, one!'

And suddenly there were not two tower blocks with their windows lit, any more. Some of the windows winked out. Some suddenly were shining brightly. They had been transformed into a huge message that was etched against the darkness.

57N 162E.

'Promise fulfilled,' she said quietly.

She waited. She thought he wasn't going to come. Then someone jumped up on the wall and sat down beside her.

Neither of them said anything for a while. They just stared at the tower blocks and their message.

'The co-ordinates of an iron camp,' he said eventually. 'I like your style.'

'It's for a place called Kamchatka. We found it on Google Earth. It's in Siberia. One of the mists leads there, doesn't it?'

He nodded. 'We'll go through it and find the camp and make them open the gates.'

She looked at him curiously. He wasn't that much older than her, and the rest were even younger.

'Can you do that? It might be a long way from the gateway. There's hardly any roads, and there's these huge volcanoes and snow and ice and forests. It's like the land before time began.'

Evan shrugged. 'We'll do it. We're wrigglers, we can do anything.'

They both kicked their heels on the wall for a bit.

'Faolan says hi,' said Evan.

Nell smiled and took something wrapped in clingfilm from her pocket. She handed it to Evan. 'Give her this from me, to say thanks. It's a bone from our dinner.'

They kicked the wall some more.

'How's Fen?' said Nell.

'Still getting treatment. Star's hopeful. She's really good. One day she'll make a good witch – oops, I mean healer.'

307

'Good.'

A silence fell. Then, 'Nell?'

She turned towards him. 'What?'

He leaned towards her and kissed her cheek. Just the lightest touch of his lips, but it took her breath away.

'What was that for?' she said, when she could talk.

He held out his hands to the street and the town. 'See, the world didn't explode. I think we can be friends.'

She watched a pulse beating quickly just below his jaw, on his throat. He wasn't as cool as he was making out. He'd felt it too. That connection between them.

She smiled. 'So, we're not enemies any more?' she said.

'I never wanted to be, believe me. When I saw you sitting on your own, eating lunch, all I wanted to do was fool around and make you smile.' He shot her a shy glance. 'And when you followed me through the woods that day, I thought you'd discovered I was Elven. And I felt scared but thrilled that a human – you – might know our secret.'

'I wish I could come with you,' she said. 'And see how this thing ends.'

Their eyes met. 'I wish you could. One day we'll be old enough to do what we want.'

Roll on that day, thought Nell.

'Do you want to give me your mobile number?' she said.

'No point. If the camp is in Kamchatka, there will be no signal.' He touched her temple. 'I'll be here. I'll think of you. Who knows when we'll meet again?'

He jumped down off the wall. The wind was blowing his hair, and that wonky grin of his was not quite as carefree as usual.

'So long,' she said, trying to keep her voice casual. 'Au revoir.'

He stopped. 'What's that about?'

She gave a reluctant smile. 'I was being Hélène. With accents. She was my inner self but I'm going to get rid of her.

'Good. I prefer Nell.'

She jumped down off the wall. 'Bye, Evan.'

'Bye, ma'elskling.'

She watched him walk away, down the alley.

'Same to you,' she called.

Ma'elskling. My precious. She put her hand to her cheek, where he'd kissed her. A fleeting contact between a girl and a boy who were never supposed to meet. Her first kiss. She smiled to herself. Friends, he'd said. Maybe, or maybe something more.

'Till next time, Evan,' she murmured, as the dark wood swallowed him.

Nell and Evan's spellbinding story continues in

FROST

Coming 2012

Read on for an exclusive extract . . .

FROST

Something woke Nell.

Heart hammering, she sat up and wrapped her old fur coat around her. She'd laid it on her bed last night for extra warmth. It still smelled of pine needles.

Something was wrong, but she didn't know what. In the darkness her radio alarm showed 6 a.m., which meant there was a long time to go before dawn.

Maybe the snowstorm had woken her – or the cold. She'd gone to bed in all her clothes, because the weather forecast had warned of temperatures down to minus ten. The New Year was two days old and it had brought a big freeze.

There it was again! Someone was throwing stones at her window.

She pulled the blind up and tried to look out, but there was frost on the inside of the glass even though the central heating had been on all night. She scraped a hole, freezing her fingertip.

A figure was standing in the garden, looking up. For a heart-stopping moment she thought it was Evan.

Evan, the mystery boy who became her friend, who wasn't human, who came from another world and rocked hers.

But it wasn't him. It was too small, and anyway he was somewhere in a wilderness far to the North. He'd been there two months and three days, and she'd begun to realize she might never see him again.

The figure waved to her, urgently, and then ran.

She pulled on her new boots and rushed out of her bedroom, stepping quickly over a boy lying on the landing, wrapped in a blanket. Her sister's door was open. She could see five bodies squashed on to Gwen's bed. Another two were on a lilo on the floor, wearing their coats.

Downstairs, she tiptoed through the living room. Each sofa had a tightly huddled couple, wrapped in quilts. The only sound, besides breathing, was faint gunfire coming from the computer by the front window. Two blanket-draped boys were slumped by it, playing some kind of game online, as though they'd been there all night.

It was party-time at Gwen's.

All her friends were crashing here, because Jackie, their mum, was working overtime. The emergency services were at full stretch because of the freak weather.

She picked her way quickly through the bodies lying on a futon on the floor, treading on a couple of them. They twitched and turned over, pulling the covers round themselves and scattering cans and bottles. There was a Post-it note stuck on the TV that hadn't been there last night. It was a threat from Mum. She must have called in during the night, whilst she was on patrol.

Gwen! Get these people out before I get back. Or else!!
I said four friends round – max!!!

Her sister was curled like a kitten in one of the armchairs. Her head came up sleepily as Nell crept by.

'Wassup? What time is it?'

'Early. Six. Go back to sleep.'

'Where you going?'

'For a walk.'

'Weirdo. You'll freeze to death.'

Gwen slumped back down and closed her eyes, but a blonde head popped up from the other armchair. Nell could just make out that it was Becca, Gwen's best friend.

'Six o'clock! Frick. I should've gone home last night! I'm working for Dad today. He'll kill me!' She began to scrabble round for her boots, treading on the sleeping bodies and making them moan horribly.

Nell fled. The front door was sealed with snow and ice and needed a kick to open it. She stepped over the Christmas tree, now lying half buried next to the wheelie bin. Her front garden and the whole of Woodbridge Road had been obliterated by the snow.

The stone thrower was waiting for her under the street lamp. She could see that it was a young girl in a fur jacket and hood, leggings and boots. A few thin white plaits peeked out from under the hood.

'Star!' said Nell, shocked. *Evan's cousin, the little witch-healer, standing in her street!*

'Can you hear?' the Elven girl cried.

'Hear what?'

But Star was off again and running down the street. Something terrible must have happened, to bring her into this world. Nell crunched and slithered after her, down the road to the church, then into the alley that led to the woods. Star was waiting at the entrance, hopping up and down impatiently, but something had caught Nell's eye. The alley was choked with snow. It had fallen last night and covered any footprints of the day before – so why was she staring at three fresh sets of prints?

The small ones were Star's. Then a bigger set. The

third looked as though it might be boots with a heel. Who wore heels in the woods, in weather like this? Someone had.

'Who else is with you?' she called.

'No one. Just me.' Star was jumping up and down, urging her on. 'Please! Can't you hear it?'

Nell listened, but she couldn't hear anything.

She wrapped her coat tight round herself, wishing she'd remembered her gloves, and ran into the woods after Star. It looked like a deadly winter wonderland, the snow lying deep between the trees, the branches etched with snow and frost.

She hadn't been back here since Evan left. She'd concentrated on her schoolwork instead and amused herself by letting her so-called friends, Paige and Bria, know that she couldn't care less about them any more.

Now she followed Star, slipping and slithering towards the hollow where the mist lay. The path down to it was a sheet of ice. She hung on to a branch as she skidded down, and got a shower of snow down her neck. Then the mist was sparkling before her like the tinsel on their Christmas tree. The stepping stones shone with ice.

Star was already dancing ahead of her, disappearing into the mist.

Nell put her foot on the first slippery stone. She could

still remember the sequence of steps that would take her through to the place that had haunted her dreams for the last two months. She'd never forget. Nor would she forget the way the mist began to thicken around her as though trying to push her back, or the feeling of vertigo as though she was walking over a chasm.

She fought her way through and emerged into the clearing. The cold was even more intense here. It hit her as though someone had left a deep-freezer door open and the tears in her eyes were turning to ice.

The clearing was deep in snow, and all around were pine trees, the ones that had scented her coat so deeply. This was the other forest, the one that was outside the world, the one that belonged to the hidden people, the Elven. This was the dangerous secret that she kept. Icicles a foot long hung from the branches and wolf tracks crisscrossed from side to side. Between the trees other patches of mist winked and twinkled at her, each one a gateway to another place.

Star was standing forlorn in the middle, her breath crystallizing in a cloud before her. Her hood was thrown back and her white plaits were shining under the Elven moon.

'I helped you,' she cried. 'Now you have to help us. There's no one else.'

Nell went over to her, sinking to her knees in the soft powder snow, and grabbed Star's hands. They were like ice. 'What is it?'

'It's happened too quickly. Can't you hear it?' whispered Star. 'Listen.'

She listened, but she couldn't hear anything. 'I don't know what you mean.'

Then her heart gave a thump. Oh Lord. That was it. *She couldn't hear anything.* There was nothing. Not even the creak and rustle of the trees now they were laden with snow. Just a silence. A deep, frozen silence.

'The Harps,' she said, horrified. 'The Harps have stopped singing.'

No more music, no more never-ending melodies from the huge devices spread through the forest, which kept the Elven land from breaking up and dying.

'The ice is spreading from the lake. And the Ice Elven are on the move.' Star's face went even paler than its normal milk-white. 'They're the bad ones, Nell! Their hearts don't beat, they're frozen.'

'What can I do?' said Nell.

Star's hands squeezed hers desperately. 'You have to go and find Evan.'

Becca made it to the shop on time. Cutler's Antique

Jewellery in the town centre was the family business. She'd left her dad parking the car, but she needn't have hurried; no one was out shopping, not in this weather.

Except for the boy sitting in the doorway, hugging his knees.

She almost didn't notice him. He was dressed in shades of pale grey, like shadows on the white snow. He blended. He had a grey hoodie with the sleeves pushed up and the zip half down as though he was hot, instead of freezing to death. There was another shade of grey for his jeans, another for his boots.

When he saw her he leaped to his feet, happy as a puppy.

'I've been waiting for you to open,' he said, brightly. He sounded slightly foreign.

Becca pulled off her fluffy beret and tucked a strand of her bed-hair behind her ear. He was definitely sweet. He was her age, maybe, or younger, and his face wasn't that special, but somehow it was startling. He had skin like a pearl, as though he'd never seen the sun. She couldn't stop staring, and when he pushed his hood back and she saw his shiny black hair, like a raven's feathers, she could hardly stop herself wanting to stroke it. She liked the style it was in. It didn't look as though he'd been to the hairdressers, or had spent hours in front of the mirror with gel. It looked like it grew that way.

His eyes were the lightest grey, too, like pale silver. He was shading them with his hand as though the day was too bright. It wasn't – in the last half hour the sky had turned purple like a bruise. There was another snowstorm on the way.

'Lots of other shops are open,' she said. 'You didn't need to sit here, freezing.'

'This one. I want this shop.' He grinned at her, eager and friendly, and wrinkled his nose. 'Let me in.'

She shouldn't – she should wait for her dad, she had to think of security. But this cute puppy-boy was hardly a threat, so she opened the door and switched off the alarm. The shop was dark, the security blinds still down. He followed her in and looked around. Their breath smoked, it seemed colder in here than outside. She switched on the electric heater.

'Aren't you cold?' she said.

Close to, his skin looked as though it was covered in a thin layer of frost that glittered.

He shrugged. 'No. I love it. Where I come from it's much colder.'

'Must be the Arctic, then.'

'Aha,' he said, in a singsong way. 'Not really. But far away.' He looked around. 'I've been wanting to come here.

It'll be fun.'

He started leaping round the place looking at the displays, cooing at the jewellery as if he was in love with gold. If Gwen and the rest of the girls were here, they'd be petting him, he was so adorable.

She went to lift the blinds.

'Don't. It's too bright. I like the darkness.'

For a moment she couldn't tell where his voice came from. She'd lost sight of him. The shop wasn't big, but she had to concentrate before she could pick him out in the gloom. He was definitely good at blending into shadows. He was standing in front of one of the display cabinets, like a child at the pick and mix, his nose almost touching the glass.

'I want that ring,' he breathed.

The object of his passion sat on a velvet cushion under a spotlight in the centre of the display, a snaky spiral of gold, with two tiny but perfect rubies for eyes.

'Right. Course you do!' She smiled at him, she couldn't help herself. As though he'd got money to buy stuff like that! 'That's the Elf ring. My dad says the goldwork is so incredibly fine and the jewels so expertly cut, it must be the work of elves.'

'Elven,' he said, absently, without taking his eyes off the ring.

'Sorry?'

'Elven, not elvish, elf or elves. It's always Elven.'

'He's only joking, it's not true,' she said, puzzled by his sudden seriousness.

He gave a start. 'Aha – of course,' he agreed, happily.

Side by side, they admired it.

'It's a serpent ring, made to coil around your finger.'

'I love it, I adore it,' he said. 'Where did you get it from?'

She didn't answer straight away because he'd picked up the black feather that her dad used to clean dust off the rings, and was brushing it absentmindedly against his white cheek. For a moment or two she was mesmerized. She wanted to keep him there, until Gwen turned up, so they could watch him together!

'This man came in a couple of years ago, and sold it to us,' she said. He was listening intently, nibbling the feather with perfect white teeth, now. 'It isn't for sale. Dad keeps it on display because he loves it.'

'Did the man give his name?' he asked.

'Yes. There's a label on the box. Look. Thorn. That's all we know.'

'Can I try it on?'

She found herself looking straight into his silver eyes. They now had a slightly tricky feline quality.

'No. Not allowed. You'll have to wait for my dad.'

He wrinkled his nose at her and looked slightly cross. Even that was sweet.

'He won't be long. Are you new round here?'

'Aha.' That seemed to be his way of saying yes.

She suddenly had a good idea. 'Well, keep it quiet, but we're having a snow party tonight. The caretaker forgot to lock the school pavilion and we're crashing there. Come along.'

He carried on looking round. 'Who's going?'

'Everyone. My bezzie mate Gwen, and the girls and—'

He whirled round, suddenly intense. '—and Nell?'

'Yeh, suppose.' For a moment she wondered how he knew Gwen's little sister, then the thought was gone. 'Anyway never mind her, you wait till you meet our gang.'

He gave a laugh. It was like ice breaking. 'Shame, but I can't. It's forbidden. I'm here for the gold, only.'

She frowned, disappointed. 'Hope you've got a lot of money, then.'

He laughed again. 'No, I'm not going to buy anything! I'm Loki Thorn. I came to get our ring back.' He looked around, his eyes alight. 'And I might as well take all the other sparkly things, too.'

Becca put her hands on her hips. Was this some kind

of joke? 'OK, so you're sweet, but really, who do you think you are?'

He carried on looking in the display cases. 'Sleep,' he said, casually, with a wave of one hand.

Becca dropped like a stone. He bent down and whispered in her ear.

'Sorry, pretty girl, but I'm your nightmare. I can make you dream whatever I want.' He leaned closer and whispered some more.

Then he began breaking the glass on all the cases, ignoring the alarm that started to sing out, shrilly. He took everything and was out of the shop before Becca's father had time to race round the corner.

As Mr Cutler later told the police, all he heard were the sounds of two people laughing and swiftly running footsteps, as the snow began to fall like a white curtain once more.